A Horse Called Blackberry

JoAnne Chitwood Nowack

A Sequel to *A Horse Called Mayonnaise*

REVIEW AND HERALD® PUBLISHING ASSOCIATION
HAGERSTOWN, MD 21740

The author assumes full responsibility for the accuracy of
all facts and quotations as cited in this book.

This book was
Edited by Gerald Wheeler
Cover designed by Willie Duke
Cover illustration by Scott Snow
Typeset: 12/13.5 Times

PRINTED IN U.S.A.

03 02 01 00   5 4 3 2

R&H Cataloging Service
Nowack, JoAnne, 1955-
    A horse called blackberry.

    I. Title.

813.54

ISBN 0-8280-1090-0

DEDICATION

To Dave and Darlene
who probably never realized
how much they were
influencing my life.

Acknowledgments

Special thanks to Jan and Jeff Polka, Jana Ruch, and Serman Hong for their dedicated efforts in manuscript preparation; to my daughter, Jennifer, for her keen insights and helpful observations in developing the story; and to my loving, patient husband, David, for his unwavering support.

CHAPTER ONE

The Florida sun, already hot for so early in the morning, baked down on Tory Butler as she ran across the field toward the Cool Springs Camp. Her long French braid slapped her back with every step. She had dreamed about this moment for months. Would Mayonnaise remember her?

As she approached the entrance to the barn she could hear someone whistling a lively tune in time to the rhythmic scrape . . . plop . . . of a shovel mucking out a horse stall. The scraping stopped and a stall door slammed. Still whistling, a stocky figure with an unruly shock of bright-red hair pushed a wheelbarrow down the corridor between the stalls.

Tory stepped into the corridor, her eyes still adjusting to the dim light of the barn's interior. Taking a deep breath, she absorbed the familiar odors of leather, horse sweat, and hay. She grinned at the man pushing the wheelbarrow. It was piled high with horse manure and old straw.

"Hello, Mike Winters," she said. "Engaging in your favorite activity, I see."

The man let go of the wheelbarrow and it hit the floor with a thud.

"Well, I'll be a monkey's uncle." He whistled in surprise. "If it isn't Tory, back from college in the big city. How are ya doin', young 'un?"

"Great, now that I'm here."

The head wrangler gave her a bear hug, then stood back and looked at her approvingly. "They must have fed you well at that school. You look strong and healthy and rarin' to tackle a summer of hard work. How 'bout it? Are you ready to be a wrangler?"

"Yep." Tory chuckled at her own understatement. Ever since the week-long horseback trip last summer when Mike and the assistant head wrangler, Brian, had asked her to come back this summer to work full time with the horses, she had thought of little else.

Tory peered around Mike at the stalls. A magnificent golden head pushed its way over the first stall door. A thick cream-colored mane framed a pair of large, intelligent eyes. The horse stretched toward Tory.

"Toby, you sweetie. You remember me, don't you?" She reached into her jeans pocket, pulled out a nub of carrot for the horse, and offered it on her outstretched palm. Toby's sticky tongue felt warm on her hand. The girl sighed. It was good to be back.

Midnight's dark face appeared over the next stall door. Tory moved to his side and smoothed her hand along the crest of his arched neck. Even in the dim light of the stable, she could see a healthy shine in Midnight's coal-black coat.

"Mike took good care of you guys over the winter, didn't he?" she murmured to the sleek gelding. "Now it's time to work for your oats."

Midnight snorted and nuzzled Tory's pocket. "Oh, you want a treat, do you? I suppose I can give you one if you promise to be good *all* summer and not run away with any campers." Tory pulled a piece of apple from her other jeans pocket and gave it to the horse.

As Tory peered into the next stall, a small mare shied into the far corner, her eyes wide with fear. She looked at least part Arabian with finely chiseled features, wide-set eyes, and flaring nostrils. Her coat had a salt-and-pepper pattern that appeared almost blue. Tory had seen such "blue roan" coloration before, but never on a horse so strikingly pretty. The creature's slender ankles moved constantly as she pranced nervously in the corner of her stall. She reminded Tory of a bird that had flown into her college dorm room through the open window during the spring, then couldn't find its way out.

"I'd love to set you free," she had crooned softly to the terrified bird, "but you're so afraid of being hurt, you won't let me close enough to help."

"This is Blackberry." Mike's voice startled her out of her thoughts. "She's a flighty one all right. Never been ridden. I don't know if we can make a trail horse out of her or not. She's really afraid of men. Been abused, I think. Blackberry was donated to the camp just a couple of weeks ago."

"Blackberry," Tory whispered, "I hope you and I can become friends."

Turning, she walked slowly down the corridor, greeting each of the horses by name. Feisty little Buckshot, the energetic bay; jug-headed Barney, the stubborn albino; beautiful princess Jasmine, the strawberry roan; Big Jim, the gentle giant; Bullet, the muscular gray steed that Brian usually rode; and Sunday and Monday, the striking paints.

"Where's Mayonnaise?" Tory asked, puzzled.

Mike laughed. "I wondered when you'd get around to asking that. He's out in the pasture. Been pining away for you." Picking up the handles of the wheelbarrow, the head wrangler started pushing it down the corridor toward the compost pile.

"Go on," Mike said as she hesitated at leaving him to do the work alone. "Go see him. The work will still be here when you get back."

She slipped out the back door of the barn and through the fence into the pasture behind the stable. Mayonnaise stood under an oak tree, contentedly swishing flies with his long tail. As she got closer, Tory could see that the horse had filled out since last summer. His chest was thicker, more muscular, and his hindquarters heavier. The tan colored "paint" pattern of his coat stood out more distinctly against the creamy white background.

"The life of a trail horse becomes you," Tory teased as she held her hand out to her old friend. Mayonnaise's ears flicked forward and he nickered softly. Tory reached into her pocket, pulled out the last carrot stub, and offered it to him.

"We're going to have some great times this summer, old boy," she whispered. "Barrel racing in the rodeo, trail riding, pack trips. You're going to be my horse for the summer. Got that?"

Mayonnaise nudged her hand with his nose, searching for another piece of carrot. The girl laughed. "You're happy as long as you're well-supplied with treats, aren't you? Well, there are plenty more where that came from." Tory began mentally planning her strategy for obtaining access to the carrot supply in the camp kitchen.

"So you're the carrot thief Simone told me about." The deep voice behind her made Tory jump. She turned to see Brian standing behind her, wearing a bright red camp shirt tucked into a pair of faded jeans. He held another red shirt in his hand.

"Have you met Simone? He's the new cook this year. He's from Jamaica. Great guy. And he was standing in the storage room when you sneaked into the cooler and got those carrots." Brian held the shirt out to Tory. His dark mustache twitched as he suppressed a smile. "Here. This is your staff shirt. They're kinda hot, but Elder Miller wants us to wear them. Of course, you could always hide in the cooler with the carrots anytime you get too warm."

Tory felt herself blush to the roots of her hair. "I didn't

steal those carrots," she said, with as much coolness in her voice as she could muster. "One of the kitchen girls told me I could get them. She didn't know where Simone was."

Brian held his hands up and laughed. "Hey, I'm sorry. I wasn't accusing you of anything. All I know is what Simone told me. Friends?" He reached out to shake her hand.

"OK." She wiped her own hand on her jeans and took his. "Friends." She wondered if he remembered that night so long ago when he had held her hand by the campfire and told her she was beautiful. If he did, she saw no sign of it now in his eyes or voice.

It's just as well, Tory thought as her eyes followed him back to the barn. *I came to camp this summer to work with the horses. I would rather not be distracted by Mr. Brian Winters.* She patted Mayonnaise's sleek neck. "You and I are going to have some adventures, aren't we?"

Just then Tory heard the distant clanging of the breakfast bell. She gave the horse a quick hug.

"Gotta go. Time for breakfast, *and* I have some business to attend to with Mr. Simone, the camp cook!"

The cafeteria looked just as she remembered it. Bright red and white checked tablecloths covered row after row of rustic picnic tables. Above the door to the serving area, the carved wooden sign announced its familiar admonition:

"Take all you want,
But eat all you take."

Tory wondered how the new cook's food would taste. She moved slowly through the line, peering over the shoulders of the staff members ahead of her, trying to see the food displayed on the serving deck.

Platters of fruit arranged in colorful geometric patterns caught her eye. Next to the fruit, a pan of steaming grits and a tray of tasty-looking vegetable omelettes set her mouth watering. "If that food tastes half as good as it looks, I'll be happy," Tory murmured to herself.

"Take my word for it, Simone is a great cook," said the young man just ahead of her in the serving line as he turned to smile at her. His dark-brown eyes twinkled with a mischievous light.

Tory remembered him from last summer. He worked with the archery team and was named Walter, but everyone called him Rob, short for Robin Hood, because of his skill with the bow and arrow. Because he was well-known throughout the camp for his flippant, irreverent attitude, Tory wondered why he even bothered to work at a Christian camp when he seemed so callous about the principles it was based on.

"You're Tory, aren't you?" Rob reached for a plate and bowl and balanced them on his tray while he fished in the silverware tray for a fork. "I remember you from the laundry last summer. I should have told you then, but I always loved the way you folded my T-shirts. You did it like my mom."

She stared at him, speechless for a moment. This didn't sound like the caustic guy she'd heard so much about last year. Had something happened to change him? "I don't know if you'd be interested or not," Rob said as he piled chunks of pineapple and cantaloupe on his plate, "but several of us have started an early morning prayer group in the chapel. We'd love to have you come if you're up for it."

"Uh . . . sure!" Tory stammered, still in shock at the difference in his attitude. "What time?"

"Six a.m." Rob flashed her a smile. "It's great. You'll love it."

Just then Simone appeared at the serving deck, carefully placing fresh, hot omelettes on the already empty tray. He looked up as Tory reached for one.

"You!" he said in his thick Jamaican accent, his dark face widening into a grin. "The carrot thief. So shameful. So shameful."

Tory hung her head, all eyes in the serving area glued on her. She wished the floor would open up and swallow her or the roof would suddenly cave in. Anything to save her from embarrassment.

Then the cook laughed heartily. "Don't look so sad, child. I was just teasing you. The girls told me they sent you into the cooler for the carrots." He leaned over the counter, holding his crisp white chef's hat in place, and whispered, "You come, girl. Anytime your horse needs a treat, you come. Simone's kitchen is open to you. Do you hear me, girl?"

She nodded. The rest of the staff in the serving line laughed as they turned their attention back to filling their plates.

Tory sighed in relief. At least she didn't have to worry about how to get special treats for the horses. She counted on them to maintain a good relationship with the animals. Suddenly she thought of the spooky little blue roan mare, Blackberry. Could she win her trust with carrots? Somehow she wasn't so sure.

CHAPTER TWO

"T ory. Over here!"

The familiar voice rose above the clatter of silverware and trays in the dining room. She maneuvered her tray through the room full of chattering staff members to the table where Mike sat. His wife, LeAnne, her short dark hair framing clear blue eyes, sat beside him as she munched on cantaloupe slices. The man grinned and waved his fork in the direction of an empty place at the table.

"Have a seat, young 'un. Have you met my better half?"

The two women smiled at each other and both nodded. Tory thought of the day last summer when she'd complained to a friend about not having a dress for an upcoming Sabbath program. Somehow LeAnne had overheard her and before the day was out, Tory returned from town with a new dress. She knew other girls for whom the head wrangler's wife had done the same thing.

"I have a good nursing job, and our home is provided here at camp," LeAnne had said when Tory protested about the dress. "God gave me some extra money to share. Consider the dress a present from Him."

They're a good match, Tory thought as she slid into the place beside LeAnne. She remembered a character in a book she'd read recently named Greatheart because of his generous spirit. *That's what Mike and LeAnne are like. They should be called the Greathearts.*

A slender girl with straight red hair and thick glasses

sat directly across the table from Tory. She stared at her plate as she ate, her shoulders hunched. The girl reminded Tory of a blackbird she'd seen hunkered on a fence wire on a frosty winter morning last January.

"Tory, this is Allie," Mike said, nodding at the red-headed girl. For a second Allie glanced up shyly and caught Tory's eye, then quickly dropped her gaze again, studying the mound of steaming grits on her plate as if it contained the secrets of the universe. "Allie is going to be the other girl wrangler at the stable this summer. You two will be getting to know each other real well."

Mike's comment reminded Tory of how much fun she'd had on the pack trip with Sandy the previous summer. It had been disappointing finding out that Sandy and Wally weren't coming back to Cool Springs Camp this summer. As she pictured Sandy's tanned face with its spattering of freckles and pert, upturned nose, Tory sighed. *Sandy, old girl, things won't be the same without you.*

None of the others at the table seemed to even notice Allie's shy behavior. Tory focused on her omelette, trying not to think about what a whole summer of working with the new girl would be like.

At least I have Mayonnaise, she told herself. She pictured herself riding the horse along the trails in the cool of the morning, the soft light of the rising sun shimmering in the dewdrops clinging to every bush and blade of grass.

"We need to have a staff meeting," Mike said, his voice pulling her back to reality. "I just need to find Brian and get him to join us."

Mike jumped up from the table and scanned the room, looking for the assistant wrangler.

LeAnne pushed back her tray, her food mostly untouched. Tory glanced at the woman's face. A vague sense of concern nibbled at the edges of Tory's mind. Something about LeAnne's skin color didn't look right.

"Are you OK?" Tory leaned over and spoke quietly, trying to avoid embarrassing her in front of the others.

"Yes, I think so," LeAnne whispered. "I'm just really excited today. You know Mike and I have been praying for a baby."

Tory smiled broadly and leaned closer to LeAnne, anxious to hear more. "No! I didn't know that." She tried to picture Mike with a baby, his work-roughened hands touching silky smooth baby skin. She was sure, boy or girl, that the little one would probably ride horses before it could walk.

"I can't have a baby of my own," LeAnne said, her eyes clouding with pain. "The doctors say I can't, that things just aren't right. So we're trying to adopt." Her face brightened.

"A call came through yesterday about a possible baby for us! We'll find out more about it today. It seems there's a prominent family in central Florida whose daughter is going to have a baby soon. The girl chose to adopt her baby out instead of getting an abortion, and she's looking for a Christian home for it."

Tory shuddered at the mere mention of the word abortion. It seemed horrible to her that a mother could even think of killing her own baby before it was born. Whoever this young girl was who was faced with the painful prospect of giving her baby away, Tory felt a rush of admiration for her decision.

Reaching over, Tory squeezed LeAnne's hand. "I'll be praying that things work out OK." She noticed Rob seated at the next table, animatedly discussing something with several other counselors. As she thought of his invitation to the early morning prayer group, she felt a familiar tug on her heart.

Father, you want me to go to that prayer group, don't you?

Mike returned to the table, Brian close at his heels.

Something lurched in the pit of Tory's stomach as she looked up to see Brooke, one of the swimming instructors, standing beside Brian.

"Uh, is it OK if Brooke sits in on this?" Brian asked, shifting his weight from one foot to the other uneasily. "She wants to help out in the stable sometimes to learn more about horses."

Her fists clenched in front of her on the table, Tory stared at her knuckles. Brooke. Tanned and willowy, with emerald-green eyes and blond hair twisted around her head like a soft crown, she looked like a goddess from some Greek myth. Tory was certain that the horses weren't the real reason the girl wanted to spend time at the barn.

"Sure, it's OK," Mike chortled and motioned for Brian and Brooke to sit down. Then he gathered up the team's empty trays and dirty plates, cups, and silverware, and headed for the dishwashing area. He grinned as he called back over his shoulder, "I'll take care of this dirty work so we can get down to *real* business."

It was just like Mike to do his share of the work and help everyone else out too. Tory had planned to take her own dishes, but the head wrangler grabbed them before she could. She glanced up at Allie and noticed a stricken look on the other girl's face.

"I should have taken those," Allie said, her voice tight. Tory almost laughed, then caught herself as she realized Allie wasn't joking. A look of fear lurked behind the girl's eyes.

"Allie," she whispered, leaning forward, "it's OK. Mike wanted to take those dishes. It's all right to let him do it."

The redheaded girl shook her head and bit her lip. Tears spilled down her pale cheeks.

Whew, Tory thought, *something must really be bothering her to make her act this way. She's like a fragile china doll. Breakable. Or maybe she's already been broken and all the pieces are just holding together on the outside.*

When Mike returned to the table he pulled a handful of lollipops from his pocket. "Dessert to help our brains work better!" He offered one to LeAnne. She gulped and shook her head. Her husband looked at her quizzically, but said nothing.

Mike cleared his throat. "I call this first wrangler staff meeting of the summer to order. Since we don't have any old business to discuss yet, we'll focus this meeting on new business and monkey business. But first we need to make sure that our business is God's business. Let's pray."

With a giggle Tory bowed her head. She loved his sense of humor. His relationship with God seemed real and alive, not serious and stuffy like some Christians she'd known.

"Father," he prayed, "we are here for just one reason—to show these campers, and even some of the other staff who don't really know You yet, what You're like. We're open for any ideas about how to do that. Thanks! In Jesus' name, Amen."

The next hour passed quickly. Mike passed out paper and pencil to each staff member and asked the group to write down three sets of goals for the summer.

"Don't write your goals for anybody else," he warned. "I want them to come from your heart. First of all, write down what you'd like to accomplish personally this summer. Make it a stretch, something you'll have to work for.

"Next, write down something you'd like the group to do together to reach out and make a difference in this camp.

"Last, but definitely not least, write down something you'd like to see God do in your life or in the life of someone close to you this summer."

Tory placed a big number one on her paper and chewed on her pencil as the group fell silent, pondering their responses. She tried to imagine what she would wish for this summer if she could accomplish anything she wanted to. All winter she'd dreamed of spending the summer working with Mayonnaise until he developed into the best trail horse in camp history. Mayonnaise was already well on his way to that goal. His training wouldn't really be a stretch for Tory, but it would be a lot of fun. Beside the number one she wrote "horse training."

The second goal presented a little more of a challenge. Tory placed a large number two on her paper and stared at it for several minutes. Finally she wrote "show Christ to the kids" beside the number. But she knew Mike wanted specific suggestions, not just concepts. She chewed on her pencil a while longer, then put down "participate in campfire programs (skits)." Just below it, she added, "teach kids through horsemanship to be kind, fair, and responsible." After thinking some more, she continued, "Have a great rodeo so kids can see that being a Christian can be a lot of fun and a great challenge."

The third goal came much more easily. Beside the large number three she wrote: "A baby for Mike and LeAnne."

"All right, time's up," Mike said at last. "The only part of your paper I want is your goals for our group. I'd like you to jot your ideas on the bottom of your paper and give it to me. The rest of it is yours to keep. It's good to always have our goals in view. They keep us headed in the direction we want to go."

Mike collected the lists of ideas and stuffed them in his jeans pocket. Tory knew he would study them later, giving each one careful consideration.

"We have one week to get the horses ready before the campers arrive," he said. "Besides working with the horses, we need to clear the riding trails, and clean up the saddles and bridles. Stable rules are the same this year as they were last year:

"No horseplay on horseback—someone might get hurt.

"Animals eat before we do—no breakfast until the horses are fed.

"A place for everything and everything in its place.

"Never give a horse a drink when he is overheated.

"Everyone takes their turn at mucking out stalls.

"Never let your horse run back to the barn.

"Always keep the feed-room door shut so the horses can't get to the grain bins.

"Any questions?"

Allie raised her hand timidly. "What time do you want us to the stables to start work each morning?" She pushed her glasses up on the bridge of her nose and cleared her throat nervously.

Tory resisted the feeling of annoyance that threatened to well up inside her. Allie's self-consciousness seemed as out of place on this team of wranglers as a ballet dancer at a rodeo. It puzzled Tory that Mike had picked Allie for a job that carried so much responsibility when she seemed so unsure of herself.

"Six a.m. sharp!" he said in answer to Allie's question. "Gettin' up with the chickens'll put hair on your chest."

Six a.m. Tory groaned to herself. *That's the time Rob's prayer group starts. I'm sure God wants me to be there, but if I don't come down when the others do, someone else will have to do my early morning chores.* She made a hasty decision and took a deep breath.

"Mike," she said quickly, before she had time to change her mind, "is it OK if I come in at 5 a.m. to get my early morning work done? I have somewhere I need to be from 6 to 7 a.m."

Although clearly puzzled, Mike still didn't hesitate.

"Sure. As long as you get your work done, it's up to you how you do it."

The rest of the group stared at her as if she'd just announced she was planning to teach Mayonnaise to fly. LeAnne shook her head. "Do you realize how early 5 a.m. is, young lady?"

Tory grinned. "I guess I'm about to find out!" She shrugged. "How bad could it be?"

CHAPTER THREE

Tory nestled on Mayonnaise's sturdy back and gazed down at the green fields and oak hammocks far below. The horse's wings beat the air slowly and majestically like those of a giant eagle surveying its domain. Suddenly a loud screeching sound filled the air. It seemed to come from every direction at once. As Tory clapped her hands over her ears to drown out the sound, she felt Mayonnaise falling . . . falling . . .

Jerking awake, she realized her alarm clock still screeched out its obnoxious wake-up call. She rolled over, moaning in pain with each movement, and pawed at the top of the clock, trying to find the snooze button. The red numbers on the front of the clock read 4:45 a.m.

"This is a bad dream," she muttered to herself. "The flying horse is real. This 4:45 a.m. stuff is the nightmare."

Sitting up on the side of her bed, she rubbed her aching muscles. "Why in the world do I hurt so much?" Then she remembered. After hours of mucking out stalls yesterday, Mike had sent her to help Brian clear a section of new trail north of the camp's airstrip. The rhythmic slashing of the old machete as she sliced through palmetto fronds was fun yesterday, but now Tory felt the strain in her back.

Tory could see the lights on in the barn as she stumbled across the archery range in the predawn darkness. She could hear Mike whistling "What a Friend We Have in Jesus" from somewhere inside the barn. Shaking her head, she wondered how anyone could be so cheerful so early in the morning.

Mike emerged from the tack room as Tory entered the corridor of the barn. He carried a hackamore on one arm and a light western saddle with the other. His round face crinkled into a grin when he saw Tory. "So you made it. Usually I'm the only one up at this hour," he chuckled. "Can't figure out why, though. It's the best time of the day to get things done."

He hung the hackamore on a peg by one of the stalls and hoisted the saddle onto the top of the stall's half door. Tory heard the thumping of hooves as the horse in the stall shied away from the saddle, crowding into its farthest corner. Without even looking into the stall Tory knew who the horse was. Only Blackberry spooked like that at the slightest excuse.

"I've already fed the horses on this side of the barn," Mike said, tossing her a plastic bucket. "You can finish up on the other side, then start helping me saddle these guys. We're going on a trail ride today."

"Trail ride? With all the horses? But the campers won't be here until next week."

He grabbed another saddle and bridle from the tackroom and headed for the far end of the barn. "A staff trail ride. We're rounding up anybody who wants to go. Counselors, lifeguards, kitchen staff . . ." His voice trailed off as he disappeared into a stall. Tory could hear him murmuring affectionately to whichever horse occupied it. She had a hunch by the tone of his voice that the horse was probably Toby or Big Jim, two of his favorites.

Filling the grain bucket, Tory carried it to the stall closest to the entrance of the barn. She looked out at the sky, the mammoth oaks silhouetted black against the silver-gray streaks of early dawn.

With a sigh, she thought, *Good job, Father. You are such an artist.*

Stocky little Merrilegs pushed his nose over the door of the first stall. Tory opened its door and his feed bin. She scratched the pony behind his ears as he shoved his nose into the feed, hungrily devouring it.

"You would think this was your first meal of this year." With a laugh she pulled playfully at Merrilegs' forelock. The sturdy little horse, with his tawny coloring and bushy mane, reminded her of a lion. She thought of last year's pack trip when Merrilegs, with Todd on his back, had outdistanced even the strongest of the bigger horses.

Mike appeared at the door of the stall. "He's a corker, that one," the man said as he slid Merrilegs' saddle onto the top of the door and hung his bridle over the saddle horn. "It was all I could do this spring to keep him out of the feed room. He's a little escape artist in reverse. Seems he can get into anything. Sometimes I think I should put a combination lock on the feed-room door and make sure he doesn't see me work the combination! We need to all keep an eye on him. If he gets into the feed bins and eats too much grain, he'll founder for sure."

Tory had seen foundered horses before and had read up on the condition in one of her horsemanship books. The book had described "foundering," or "laminitis," as a condition of congestion and fever in the feet caused by eating too much rich, high-protein food. One of the foundered horses Tory knew of never fully recovered from the lameness. Its hooves grew out in a strange curled pattern that made walking difficult.

"I don't want that to happen to you." Tory gave Merrilegs one last pat and turned to go. She double-checked the latch on the outside of the stall door to make sure it was secure.

In just a few minutes she finished feeding all the

horses on her side of the barn. Then she turned her attention to saddling the horses that had finished eating. She grabbed a curry comb and hoof pick on her way to the stall directly across from Merrilegs. As she approached the door Mayonnaise's head appeared, reaching out for a treat. "Sorry, boy. No treat this morning. It was all I could do to get out of bed and get down here."

Slipping into the stall, she began brushing Mayonnaise down, taking care to always brush in the direction of hair growth to keep from tickling his sensitive skin. Next she grabbed his hooves one at a time by the hair just below the fetlock and tugged gently, making soft clucking noises to let Mayonnaise know that she wanted him to lift his foot. With the hoof pick she cleaned horse manure and debris from around the frog of each hoof and under the inside edges of his horseshoes.

"You are absolutely wonderful," Tory whispered in the gelding's ear. "There's no horse on earth more gentle and obedient than you are."

Placing the saddle blanket high on Mayonnaise's withers, she slid it down onto his back in the direction of hair growth. She didn't want twisted hairs to irritate him all day. Then she flipped the right stirrup and the cinch of Mayonnaise's saddle up over the seat and heaved the saddle up onto his back. The horse stood perfectly still while Tory reached under his belly to grab the cinch and pull the leather cinch strap through it. Since it would be hours before the trail ride she left it a little loose for now. She slipped the bit of Mayonnaise's bridle into his mouth and the headstall up over his ears, fastening the throatlatch securely.

"There." Tory surveyed her work with satisfaction. "You're the best-looking trail horse this side of the Rockies."

Mayonnaise snorted and nudged her arm with his nose. "OK, OK," she giggled, "the other side of the Rockies, too."

Just then Tory glanced at her watch. "Uh, oh. Gotta go, old boy. It's 5 minutes to 6:00. Time for my prayer group." After patting Mayonnaise's neck she hurried to the tack room where Mike stood, sorting through the extra bridles.

"The bridle Jasmine's been using just doesn't fit her right." He shook his head. "Not good. She needs a good bridle—she has a sensitive mouth, you know."

Even though she knew Mike was talking more to himself than to her, Tory nodded. She was sure that he would continue on the same way even if no one was there to listen.

"I've got to go. The horses are all fed and Mayonnaise is saddled. I'll be back in an hour to help finish up. OK?"

Mike looked up from the bridles and smiled. "OK, kid. Have fun doing whatever it is you're doing. I'll see you in an hour."

"It is a prayer group," she said, feeling suddenly self-conscious. "Rob invited me. It sounded like a good thing."

"Can't think of anything better." Mike gave her the thumbs up sign. "But you better skedaddle or you'll miss it."

Tory loved the camp chapel with its octagonal shape and its wraparound picture windows. It was rustic but very comfortable, a great location for an early morning gathering.

Rob sat on the floor near the raised platform at the front of the chapel. He looked up and smiled when he heard her come through the door.

"Glad you could make it, Tory. There are some others planning to be here too. But even if it's just you and me, it'll be great. There's something about coming out in the early morning to pray together." He laughed. "I guess God knows how hard it is for us to drag ourselves out of bed and gives us an extra blessing if we're willing to do it!"

As Tory nodded she remembered how she had felt when her alarm went off at 4:45. She sat down on the floor beside Rob. As he talked about God she noticed how his face lit up. He was clearly a different person than the Rob she'd known last year.

"Tell me to back off if I'm being too nosey," she said, watching him leaf through the study Bible in his lap, "but you seem so different now than last summer. What happened to you?"

Rob chuckled. "I can't think of any question I'd rather answer than that one. But I see the others arriving now, and we need to get started. Could we take a trail ride one evening this week and I'll tell you about it?"

"Sure!" Tory stuck her hand out to shake his. "It's a deal."

Two guys came in first. Tory recognized one of them as Brett, a lifeguard. She'd never seen the other one. His blond hair had a bleached out look like Brett's, probably also from long hours in the water under the searing Florida sun.

The guys had just settled in when three girls entered and quickly found places on the floor. Tory had met one of the girls, a counselor named Breeze, her first day at camp. She was a pretty girl with short black hair and a soft, whispering voice. Tory hoped she would have a chance to get to know her better during the summer. She'd seen the other two girls at mealtime in the cafeteria, but had no idea who they were.

Rob greeted each person by name as they sat down. Tory listened carefully and made a mental note of each of their names. The guy with Brett, Rob called Paul. The two girls with Breeze were Jennifer and Vanessa. Jennifer's shoulder length sandy blond hair framed a tanned face with perfect features. Vanessa had fair skin with golden brown freckles, even white teeth, and a cascade of bright red hair.

Rob introduced Tory to the rest of the group. Then he opened the meeting with a short prayer, asking for God's presence to be with them during the next hour.

"I'm absolutely convinced," he said when he finished, "that prayer is the key to having a real and powerful connection with God. We talk *about* God, study *about* God. These things are important, but how much time do we actually spend in direct communication with Him? It's by being *with* someone that we learn about them and they have an influence in our lives."

Tory nodded in agreement. What he said made sense to her, and the look of peace and purpose in his face as he spoke made his message that much more powerful.

"God wants us to talk to Him," Rob continued. "Not just a 'canned' prayer about the missionaries across the sea, but a constant conversation about everything that's important to us. He wants to be our Best Friend. He wants us to ask Him to work in every situation in our lives because it gives Him another opportunity to show us how much He cares about us."

"Sometimes God says 'no' when we ask Him for something," Vanessa said. "But I guess it wouldn't be very loving of Him to give us everything we want, especially if it would be bad for us in the long run."

Breeze laughed, her silvery voice rippling like waves on the seashore. "That reminds me of my grandma. When I was a little girl, she told me that my life is like a big tapestry and every day God is weaving a beautiful pattern on the front of it. All I can see from my side, though, are the knots and tangled threads and a few of the colorful patches, but never like He views it. She told me to go ahead and talk to God about how tangled the threads look to me. Grandma said I could even ask Him to use a different color or stitch if I wanted to, but that I should remember to trust Him with the pattern. Because someday, when He turns the tapestry over and lets me see the other side, I'd be glad He did it just the way He did."

"Great illustration," Rob grinned at her. "I've got

some tangled threads I'd like to talk to Him about today. How about you guys?" Tory nodded with the rest and joined him as he knelt to pray. A rush of excitement flooded through her as she thought about being a part of this unusual group of people. Breeze intrigued her. Tory determined to take the time to get to know her better. And Rob—what could have happened to make such a change in his life? She hoped she wouldn't have to wait long to find out.

CHAPTER FOUR

Mayonnaise stood placidly by the hitching rail with Big Jim and Jasmine as Tory hurried down the path from the chapel. Mike emerged from the barn leading Toby.

"All right! Tory's back," he called to the others. "We'll get these horses saddled before breakfast yet."

As she entered the barn, she noticed Blackberry's saddle and bridle untouched on her stall door. Approaching the stall, she peered inside. The mare stood trembling in the corner, her ears flicking nervously toward each new sound. Tory slid the door latch open and cautiously entered the stall.

"It's OK, girl," she murmured, keeping her voice low and even. She started toward the mare. With the speed of a striking snake, Blackberry wheeled and kicked out at her, catching her on the left shin. Wincing in pain, Tory flattened herself against the wall farthest from the horse. Then she inched along it until she reached the door, quickly opened it, and slipped out of the stall, almost bumping into Brian.

"Whew, I don't think I'll do that again," she said, sinking down onto the floor of the corridor. She pulled her jeans leg up and looked at her shin. The skin wasn't broken but a reddened area marked the spot where Blackberry's hoof had struck her. Tory knew she'd have a nasty bruise there by tomorrow.

"What happened?" Brian stopped to examine her injury. He whistled in amazement at the hoofmark. "She really got you, didn't she? She's going to be a handful. Too bad she's been mistreated. I don't know if she'll ever trust humans again." He shook his head. "I don't envy you the job of breaking her in."

She stared at him. "Me? Who said *I* was the one who's going to do it?"

"Didn't you know? I thought Mike talked to you about it."

Just then the head wrangler emerged from one of the stalls at the far end of the barn, Big Dan, the Belgian, in tow. "What's going on here?" he asked, looking from Brian to Tory. "Are you OK?"

"Just a little bruise." She pulled her pant leg back down. "Blackberry kicked me. I went in to saddle her. I didn't realize she'd never been saddled before."

"Nope." Mike shook his head. "She's green as grass. I put the saddle up there on her stall door to get her used to its smell."

Mike gave Big Dan's reins to Brian and motioned for him to lead the mammoth horse out to the hitching rail.

"Tory," Mike said, a serious tone in his voice, "I want you to be the one to work with Blackberry. She needs a gentle, experienced rider. Someone she can learn to trust. Will you do it?"

Tory ran her hand over the growing bump on her shin. If there was anything she hated in life, it was being kicked or bitten by a horse. She thought of Mayonnaise's impeccable manners and how much she'd looked forward to working with him this summer. At the same time she knew that taking on Blackberry's training would consume all her time and energy.

"What about Mayonnaise?"

"I'd like Allie to work with him," he said, lowering his voice. "It'd be a good confidence builder for her."

Tory's heart sank, but she tried not to let her disappointment show. She trusted his sixth sense when it came to matching horses and riders, even if she didn't understand his decisions at first.

"OK." Tory stood and brushed the sand from her jeans. "I'll work with Blackberry."

"Good. You can start whenever you're ready."

Right after breakfast Tory hurried back to the barn to do last-minute preparations for the trail ride. She checked the cinch strap on each saddle for the proper snugness by shoving two fingers between the girth strap and the horse's belly. If the strap was too tight to admit two fingers, she loosened it a little. But if the strap easily allowed two fingers between, she tightened it. She didn't want anyone's saddle slipping under the horse's belly out on the trail.

Allie stood by Mayonnaise, smoothing the tangles from his mane with a metal currycomb. Tory pretended not to notice, but she felt a tightening in her chest, as if someone in heavy boots was standing on it. The feeling triggered a memory of that day years before when her mother had brought her new little sister home from the hospital. Strangely, now she felt the same sense of loss, of being replaced, that she had experienced then. She knew her days of having Mayonnaise to herself were over.

"Tory, could you check Mayonnaise's cinch, too?" Allie asked, her voice apologetic. A wave of annoyance swept over Tory. How could Allie function as a staff wrangler if she didn't even know how to check a saddle cinch strap?

"I'm sorry you won't be able to work with Mayonnaise this summer," the girl said softly as Tory inspected the strap and tightened it slightly. Tory ran her hand up along Mayonnaise's crest and scratched him behind his left ear.

"It's OK," Tory said with more conviction that she felt. "You'll do great with him. He's a good horse." Suddenly she realized that Allie could have tightened her own cinch strap. Was the strap just an excuse the girl used to let her know she understood how hard it was to lose Mayonnaise?

"Thanks, Allie." Tory looked her straight in the eye this time. "I'm glad you're the one who'll be training him. Let me know if I can help you."

The other girl grinned and nodded. Her whole face lit up when she smiled.

She's really pretty, Tory thought. *And nice. Maybe we'll have fun working together this summer after all.*

A commotion on the archery field caught Tory's attention. A group of camp staff members, led by a counselor named Jake, charged toward the stable. Tory remembered Jake from last summer. He and Rob had been best friends then. Jake had the same irreverent, flippant attitude that Rob used to have. Now Jake's name held an honored spot at the top of Rob's prayer list.

"This could be scary," Tory said. Allie followed her gaze to the ragtag bunch making their way across the field. Jake wore an old floppy Stetson and high-heeled western boots. A red bandanna flapped from his jeans pocket. Several of the others wore cowboy hats too.

"Would you look at that," Allie whistled softly. "A real herd of cowpokes."

Tory giggled. Here was a side of the girl she'd never seen. "Come on, Allie," she said, still smiling. "We've got our work cut out for us this morning."

Mike and Brian joined the girls just as the other staff members arrived at the hitching rail. The head wrangler began assigning horses, and Brian moved from one rider to the next, quietly instructing each of them in the basics of horsemanship and the special characteristics of each horse. Tory and Allie followed his lead.

With amusement Tory noticed that Mike matched up Jake with Barney, the albino. Jake stood at Barney's left side, his right boot in the stirrup, puzzling over how to swing up into the saddle. Barney craned his head around and gazed at his rider with his bright pink eyes. Tory hurried to Jake's side.

"Barney's wondering how you're going to mount up that way," she said, smiling. "Try the other foot in the stirrup. The rest will be a lot easier."

Abruptly Jake pulled his right foot from the stirrup. "I haven't done a lot of riding," he mumbled. He placed his left foot in the stirrup. "Now what?"

"Grab the saddle horn with your left hand and at the same time, bounce your weight off your right foot and swing your right leg up and over the saddle. Do it all in one smooth motion." Tory held Barney's reins to steady him and motioned for Jake to try it. "Go ahead. It's easy."

Jake grasped the saddle horn and swung into the saddle, then grinned at her with a look of triumph on his face. "Just call me the Lone Ranger," he said, straightening his Stetson.

She laughed. "There's a little more to learn before you're ready to take off across the prairies. Do you know how to neck rein a horse?"

"No." He looked crestfallen, then his face brightened. "But I can learn. Give me a quick crash course, OK?"

Tory led Barney, with Jake in the saddle, into the rodeo arena beside the stable. She wasn't worried about the horse running away with him, but the animal had such a stubborn streak in him that he'd refuse to work if he thought there was even a remote chance he could get out of it. He knew when Tory took him to the arena, however, that she meant business.

"Barney responds to your hands on his reins and to your legs on his sides," she explained. "Squeeze your legs gently into his sides, lean forward a little, and make a clucking noise with your tongue when you want Barney to go. Pull back evenly on both reins when you want him to stop. Say 'Whoa' in a firm voice. Make sure he comes to a full stop when and where you want him to. You're in charge here, not him. You both need to understand that."

Jake nodded, listening intently. "OK. Gotcha so far. Now, how do I turn him?"

Tory stood beside Barney's left shoulder and grasped his reins just above Jake's hands. "This is the tricky part. If you want him to turn right, lay the reins over the left side of his neck, like this." She pulled them over to show him just how much pressure to apply. "At the same time, press Barney's right side with your heel. Works like a charm if the horse you're riding is well trained. And Barney is."

Letting go of the reins, Tory stepped back to give Jake room to practice. He maneuvered Barney back and forth across the corral. To Tory's relief, the horse responded co-operatively. "Great job, Jake," she said as he reined the horse into a figure-eight pattern.

He flashed her a quick smile. "I'm a fast learner. You can let me out of the cage now. I think Barney and I have an understanding."

Tory opened the gate to the arena and stood back to let rider and horse pass. She gave Jake the thumbs up sign. "OK, cowboy. Now's your chance to prove yourself. The trail ride is heading out right now. Just pull in behind Big Jim there."

Jake nodded, an intent expression on his face as he reined Barney into his place in the line. He waved a "thank you" to Tory.

She glanced around the hitching area, wondering which horse Mike wanted her to take out this time. Allie was already riding Mayonnaise up and down the line of riders, checking for problems. The gentle gelding seemed to have a calming, steadying effect on the girl. And Allie's sensitive hands brought out the best in Mayonnaise. They were clearly a good match.

Only Old Henry remained tied to the hitching rail. Tory patted the ancient horse's neck affectionately. "I'm surprised you made it through the winter, old boy," she murmured. "How about a trail ride?" She remembered her first trail ride the previous summer and how mortified she'd been at being stuck with Old Henry. Now she actually looked forward to riding him.

Just as Tory swung up into Henry's saddle, she saw Brooke on Jasmine inching her way up the line of riders toward Brian. She looked the part of the perfect cowgirl from her black boots to her striking western shirt and black hat. Tory turned her attention to the riders in the back of the line so she wouldn't have to watch the girl's obvious attempts to get Brian's attention.

"All right, let's head out," Mike shouted from his perch on Big Jim's back. "Brian will lead and I'll pick up the rear with Tory and good Old Henry."

The long line of horses moved slowly down the airstrip toward the trail leading to the river. Tory felt a sense of excitement welling up inside her. She closed her eyes and soaked in the sunshine, listening to the sound of the grasshoppers whirring through the tall grass. It was a perfect day for the first trail ride of the season.

She wondered how long it would take to get Blackberry ready to go out with the other horses. Unconsciously she ran her hand over the knot forming on her shin where the horse had kicked her. Would the little roan mare ever trust her enough to even let her get close to her?

CHAPTER FIVE

A gray squirrel chattered nervously as the rowdy group of riders, led by Brian on Bullet, pushed along the narrow path cut through thick scrub oak and underbrush. Brooke followed close behind on Jasmine. Bullet danced and side-stepped, anxious to break into a gallop, sometimes crowding back into Jasmine.

Tory watched Brian from the back of the line. She admired his skill in keeping Bullet under control while at the same time he scouted out the trail and kept an eye on the riders following him. When Bullet brushed against Jasmine, Brian appeared embarrassed and apologetic. Brooke beamed each time it happened, clearly enjoying the situation.

Tory recognized the spots on the trail she and Brian had cleared on their trailblazing expedition. The next section of trail would circle around the Indian village, along the river, then out onto the airstrip and back to the barn. One short section of the trail had been only recently constructed. Tory wondered how the horses would respond to a totally different path.

They're such creatures of habit, she mused. *Anything new and different frightens them. Sort of like humans sometimes.* She thought of Allie and how hard it must have been for her to come to camp as a wrangler without knowing anyone but Mike and LeAnne. *Whatever the girl carries around with her, I'll have to admit she's got courage.*

Mike reined Big Jim up close beside Old Henry. "Hey, kiddo, how's it going?"

"Great!" Tory grinned. "You and I are both up here close to the treetops on these two, aren't we?"

The wrangler laughed. "Sky riders. That's what we are." He nodded at the line of horses and riders plodding along ahead of them. "Pretty good for the first trail ride of the season, huh? Like a bunch of grandmas in rocking chairs. That's the way we like our trail rides. Calm and uneventful."

The trail opened into a clearing bordered by oaks and mulberry trees. A group of Indian tepees clustered around a large fire pit in the center of the clearing. Mike motioned toward it. "The campers love coming here for campfires. We need a great Indian story to act out for them this summer. Know any good ones?"

Tory pondered a few moments, then suddenly remembered a story one of her teachers in church school had shared with her several years before. "I know one," she said, her voice rising in excitement. Henry flicked his ears back toward her, listening. "It's a true story about a wagon train, Indians, kidnapping, a ransom, and answered prayer."

Mike's eyes widened with interest. "Sounds like just the story for us. Will you share it with the group next staff meeting?"

"Sure." Her mind raced as she pictured Brian, Allie, and Mike acting out the scenes of the story. "We'll need a baby, to be kidnapped by the Indians. And two young-looking guys to be the two boys in the story."

"I wish LeAnne and I could help you in the baby department." His face clouded with sadness. "Our adoption fell through. We found out this morning."

Tory bit her lip. "I'm sorry, Mike. You and LeAnne must be terribly disappointed."

"Yeah." He sighed and patted Jim's massive neck. "It's hardest on LeAnne. I've got the horses to take my attention. It's like having a whole stable of kids. And the campers are great, too. But LeAnne was really counting on getting that baby. She's pretty upset."

Tory's thoughts flashed back to the prayer group that morning. Kneeling there on the chapel floor, holding hands in a circle, she and the others had presented Mike and LeAnne's desire for a baby to God. She'd been sure then that the adoption would go through. But now . . . Had God even heard their prayer?

Mike pulled Big Jim back into line behind Henry. He and Tory rode along in silence. The trail narrowed and veered away from the Indian village toward the river. Tory watched the horses ahead of her perk up their ears. Their nostrils flared as they caught the scent of water.

"The river!" Brian shouted, and urged Bullet into a canter. The rest of the horses surged forward, anxious to reach the cool water. Even stolid Barney perked up. Tory smiled to herself as she watched Jake using the leg signals he had just learned that morning.

The river's coffee color looked dark and uninviting compared to the camp's crystal-clear spring, but the horses stretched their necks eagerly to gulp the cool water. Tory loosened Henry's reins and let him wade out into the river.

As Henry drank, Tory propped her legs up on the cantle of the saddle, relaxing in the sunshine. Out of the corner of her eye she could see Brian just downstream from her. He held Bullet's reins taut as the horse pawed the water and snorted. Knowing that Bullet would plunge out into the current and swim without a moment's hesitation, she was glad Brian held him back. Other horses with less experienced riders might try to follow Bullet's example should he start swimming. It could be a recipe for disaster with lunging, slippery horses and panicking riders.

All at once Tory felt Henry shift his weight beneath her. His hind quarters dropped slightly. Before she could think of what to do next, the horse threw himself into the water and started to roll.

"Henry!" she shrieked as she toppled into the river. Instantly she thrashed in the shallow water, trying to gain her footing and avoid Henry's flailing legs. The horse rolled back over and stood up before she did, shaking himself from head to foot, like a dog after a bath.

Grabbing Henry's reins, Tory pulled herself to her feet amid roars of laughter from the rest of the staff. As she pushed dripping strands of hair out of her face, she looked up to see Brian, collapsed in a heap on Bullet's back, tears of laughter streaming down his cheeks. Mike slapped his legs, saying over and over, "I can't believe it. I didn't know the old feller had it in him."

Tory led Henry out of the river, laughing along with the others. Her boots squeaked with every soggy step. Rivulets flowed from Henry's saddle blanket. Tory wrung as much moisture as she could from her saturated T-shirt, then sat down to pour the water from her boots.

"Henry, Henry, Henry," she scolded. "You really know how to disrupt a person's life."

The horse swung his head around and gazed at Tory with an innocent expression in his rheumy old eyes.

"Oh, don't give me that virtuous look," she said in mock severity. Her jeans felt like wet plaster on her legs, but she clambered back up into the saddle. She turned her face toward the sun, thankful for its warmth on her skin.

"OK. Let's head on down the trail," Brian said to the group. He caught Tory's eye and grinned broadly, giving her the thumbs up sign of approval. Tory smiled back just as Brooke pulled Jasmine into line beside him. Brooke glanced at Brian, then at Tory, a worried look on her face.

Tory reined Henry onto the trail. The image of Brooke's expression danced in her mind. Could Brooke's whole self-concept be wrapped around Brian's opinion of her?

I refuse to do that to myself, Tory thought, suddenly feeling sorry for Brooke. Brian seemed to have so many girls who followed him around. Tory remembered the last night of the pack trip the previous summer when Brian had told her how beautiful she looked in the moonlight. Did he use that line on every girl he knew? She made a mental note to make sure he never had the chance to use it on her again.

Mike pulled Big Jim in behind Tory and Henry. The muscles in his jaw twitched as he tried to keep a straight face, but one look at Tory's soggy saddle sent him into another gale of laughter. Tory pretended to be insulted, crossing her arms and thrusting out her lower lip in an exaggerated pout.

"See if I ever speak to you guys again," she said, including the snickering riders just ahead of her. "Making fun of my misfortune. Fair-weather friends, that's what you are."

The trail zigzagged through the scrub toward the airstrip. The newly cleared section lay just ahead, the last stretch before the open path along the edge of the field to the stable. Mike pushed ahead of Jim, maneuvering his way to the front.

"I want to check out this new trail before we ride on it," he announced as he joined Brian at the head of the column of riders. Tory knew he was watching for sharp sticks and branches that could cut the horses' legs and possibly spook them.

Halfway along the new section of trail Tory noticed an odd buzzing sound that seemed to fill the air. Suddenly Bullet squealed and reared back, almost throwing Brian into the brush. Jasmine snorted and stamped her feet. Brooke screamed, slapping at her neck and arms.

"Yellow jackets," Brian shouted. "I just rode over their nest. *Run!*"

Barney, right behind Jasmine, shied to the side of the trail. Jake covered his face with his hands, trying to protect himself from the angry insects. Tory watched in horror as the yellow jackets swarmed over his arms, neck, and back. It was as if they had chosen him as the special object of their wrath.

Brian kicked Bullet into a gallop and let him run full-speed toward the airstrip. Jasmine crashed through the brush, Brooke clinging tightly to her back, her eyes wide with fear. Some of the other horses followed her.

Tory cut through the brush, too, trying to avoid the yellow jackets' nest. A few buzzed around her, but none of them tried to sting her. Henry seemed oblivious to the commotion. Even when Midnight backed into him to avoid being kicked by the horse ahead, Henry never flinched. He just plowed through the brush, headed for home.

"Dear God, please don't let anyone be allergic to bee stings," Tory whispered. "Especially Jake." She had no idea how many stings he actually had, but she knew it was enough to cause a serious reaction in his body.

"I'm going to find LeAnne," Tory shouted to Mike. "She'll know what to do for the stings." Mike nodded and waved her on.

Tory squeezed her heels into Henry's flanks and clucked to him, asking for more speed. Henry's ears perked up. Tory could feel his whole body respond to her request. He seemed to sense the urgency of his mission.

"Good boy." She leaned forward and gave Henry his head. Never had she seen the old horse so energetic. "Just don't have a heart attack on me."

Once on the airstrip, Tory urged Henry into a gallop. His mane whipped her face as they raced past the tennis courts and the archery range. The old horse tried to veer into the stable area, but Tory reined him past the barn to Mike and LeAnne's little flat-topped bungalow.

"LeAnne!" she shouted, pulling Henry to a stop in front of the house. The horse's sides heaved and white lather covered his bony chest. Tory jumped down stiffly, her wet jeans pasted to her skin.

The door to the bungalow flew open and LeAnne appeared, her face white. "What is it? Who's hurt? Is it Mike?"

"Yellow jackets," Tory gasped. "I think Mike's OK. But Jake has lots of stings. Can you come?"

The woman ran back inside, not bothering to close the door. She returned a short time later with a bowl full of baking soda mixed with water and carried a first aid kit in her other hand.

"Who knows what we'll need," she said. "Better to have it all there just in case."

With a nod Tory followed her toward the barn. The nurse stopped at the end of the hitching rail and set up a treatment area on the ground.

"Well, the first victim should be here any second," LeAnne said, glancing at her watch. "Every one of those horses will head for the barn if you give them their way. They'll get here a whole lot faster than we could get out to the airstrip where they are."

Just then Barney galloped into the barn lot, Jake hanging onto the saddle horn. The horse swung around to the hitching post and stopped abruptly. Tory ran to his side, reaching up for his hand.

"Come on, Jake," she said. "Let's check out those stings."

Trembling and barely able to stand, Jake dismounted. LeAnne hurried over to help support him and together she and Tory got their first patient to the makeshift clinic.

"Whew!" LeAnne whistled in amazement as she counted the welts on Jake's trunk, neck, face, and arms. "Twenty-seven stings! It's a good thing you're not allergic."

Jake groaned. "Just my luck. My first trail ride and I

get attacked by killer insects. Maybe horseback riding is too dangerous for a city boy like me!"

Tory smeared baking soda paste on each of his stings. "Come on, Jake, a little danger is good for the soul. Right, LeAnne?"

When she glanced at the woman she saw immediately that something was wrong. LeAnne was doubled over, holding her stomach and moaning, her skin a ghastly gray.

Help me Father, Tory prayed.

"Jake, watch her," she ordered. "I'm going after Mike."

CHAPTER SIX

Tory looked wildly around the hitching area. Which horse should she take? She knew she had to reach Mike quickly. Henry stood with his head hanging almost to the ground, his sides heaving. He had already given every ounce of energy he had to get her here. She couldn't ask more of him.

The only other horse in the hitching area was Barney. Tory grabbed his reins, untied them, and deftly flipped them over his head. Then she leaped into the saddle and leaned down close to his neck, squeezing both legs into his sides. Feeling the horse's muscles tighten in response to her signals, she reined him away from the hitching rail and onto the trail toward the airstrip.

Once in the open with a clear path ahead, Tory urged Barney into a dead run. The horse stretched out low, his hooves pounding the sandy ground as he ran. Tory flattened herself against Barney's neck. His long white mane whipped her face in stinging lashes. Tears streamed down her cheeks, blurring her vision.

Several large shapes loomed ahead. Tory recognized first Jasmine and Midnight. Then followed several other horses, all with riders intact. Tory knew Mike wouldn't leave the area of the yellow jacket nest until every rider was safely away.

Miraculously, Barney didn't swerve or try to turn back to the stable as he met the other horses. "Good boy," she cheered the horse on. "You're not so barn bound and stubborn after all."

Mike and Brian stood beside their horses at the edge of the field where the new trail emerged. They both looked up, startled expressions on their faces as Barney galloped toward them.

"Mike!" Tory shouted, her throat burning and her breath coming in short gasps from the strenuous ride. She pulled Barney to a stop just in front of them. "It's LeAnne. Something's wrong with her. You've got to go."

Without hesitation, Mike swung up into Big Jim's saddle and headed down the airstrip for the barn. Tory stared in amazement at the massive horse's speed. His huge hooves slammed the ground like cannonballs.

Brian swung up onto Bullet's back and nodded to Tory. "Everyone's out of the woods," he said. "What a fiasco! I'm just thankful no campers were involved in this ride. What's going on with LeAnne?"

"I don't know. She just got real sick and almost passed out. I left her with Jake while I came to get Mike. She's looked sick ever since I got here this summer. But this is lots worse. Something's wrong." Tory turned Barney back toward the stable. "I want to get back and check on her."

"I'll go with you." Brian reined Bullet in beside her. The gray gelding arched his neck regally as he pranced along, eager to run. Tory admired the gentle, easy way Brian held his horse in perfect control. They rode along quietly for a few minutes.

"Tory, there's something I need to talk to you about," Brian said, breaking the silence. His voice sounded tight and distant as if he were roping his words and pulling them out against their will. "Maybe this isn't a good time since we're both worried about LeAnne and this disastrous trail ride, but I need to tell you how I feel about you . . ."

He stared down the airstrip, voice trailing off. She

looked up to see Brooke on Jasmine riding back toward them, then glanced back at Brian to see his face flushed under his tan.

"I need to go. I want to make sure LeAnne is OK," Tory said quietly. She kicked Barney into a canter, keeping her eyes straight ahead as she passed Brooke on the path. Whatever Brian had to say, she wasn't sure she wanted to hear it. And whatever game Brooke was playing, she didn't want to participate.

Mike's station wagon pulled out of the stable hitching area just as Tory trotted Barney up to the rail. LeAnne sat slumped in the front passenger seat, her head resting against the door frame, eyes closed. Mike waved and yelled out the window, "Be back later. Just get the horses put away."

Jake emerged from the barn, crumbly white patches of baking soda paste still stuck on his skin. He grinned when he saw Tory.

"I don't think I've ever seen such wild riding," he said, shaking his head. "You really know how to get the most unlikely horses to give all they've got for you."

She slipped down from Barney's back. "Thanks, Jake. It's amazing what we all can do when we have to. I saw you doing some pretty good riding today, too. Are you feeling OK with the stings and all?"

He shrugged. "They don't feel great, but the baking soda is helping. Hopefully they won't swell up too much."

Loosening the cinch on Barney's saddle, Tory led him out into the field beside the corral to cool him down. Jake walked along beside her, chewing on a stalk of grass.

"I'm really worried about LeAnne," he said. "She looked pretty sick when she left here."

Tory looked at him in surprise. She could hear the genuine concern in his voice. It contrasted sharply with the self-absorbed, callous attitude she'd seen in him every other time she'd been around him.

"I'm worried, too." Tory paused and turned to face Jake. "I'd really like to pray for her. Would you pray with me?"

Jake stared at the piece of grass in his hand and shifted uneasily from one foot to another.

"That's OK," she said quickly. "I didn't mean to put you on the spot. It just helps me a lot to hand over whatever is worrying me to God."

He looked up and met her gaze. She could see the confusion in his eyes. "How do you know God even hears you?" Jake threw the piece of grass down. "He's never answered any of my prayers. I'm not sure He even exists."

Tory led Barney to the shade of one of the huge oak trees in the field and sat down. Jake lowered himself down beside her. She sensed his need to talk.

"It sounds like you've had some rotten things happen in your life," she said. "Do you want to talk about it?"

He wrapped his long arms around his legs, resting his chin on his knees. For a long time he sat like a statue. The only sounds were the crunching of grass as Barney grazed and a bird's constant chirping in the tree above them. Tory waited quietly, knowing he would either start talking or get up and walk away. She remembered Rob's comment about Jake as he requested special prayer for him this morning.

Jake's struggling right now, Rob had said. *He's been really hurt, and I think he blames it on God. I know how that feels because that's where I was just last year. All the obnoxious behavior is just a cover-up for a lot of hurt.*

With a sigh Jake closed his eyes and began moving gently back and forth as if he were rocking a little child.

"My dad's an elder in our church," he said finally. "Everyone thinks he's such a spiritual giant. He's really nice when other people are around, but it's different when they're not." He stopped rocking, opened his eyes, and stared at her. The look of cold hatred in his eyes sent chills up her spine.

"If God's anything like him, I don't want anything to do with Him." Jake spat the words out like they were something rotten.

Her thoughts tumbled over one another as she listened, wondering what Jake's father had done that had hurt his son so much. She'd met the man once at the end of last summer when he came to camp to pick Jake up. He'd been friendly then, going out of his way to meet his son's friends. Neither he nor Jake had given any clue that anything was wrong in their family.

Barney tugged on the reins in an attempt to munch a tuft of grass just out of reach. Tory released the end of the reins and let him be free to move around. He wouldn't stray away. The horse was far too mesmerized by the crunchy clover at his feet. She sighed, thankful that Barney wouldn't distract Jake when he needed to talk.

Jake closed his eyes again and leaned back against the tree. When he spoke again, his voice sounded old and tired.

"Ever since I can remember, my dad has seemed to be like two people. He's really religious and talks a lot about God. You'd think when he teaches a class at church or preaches a sermon that he's the best Christian in the world.

"But as soon as no 'outsiders' are watching, he changes. I've seen him hit my mom lots of times. It's like she can't do anything right. He'll go on and on about something she did or didn't do, then he'll start yelling and hitting her. Once he even held a knife to her throat, saying he was going to kill her."

Tory gasped in horror. "What do you do when he's like that? It must be terrible!"

"When I was little, I'd try to hide," Jake said, his face grim. "Sometimes he'd pick me up and throw me across the room or kick me. Now that I'm older and bigger than him, he doesn't dare. But I worry a lot about my mom. And my little sister. What kind of life is that for them?"

"I'm sorry, Jake" Tory reached over and touched his shoulder. She could feel his body trembling as if he were sobbing inside, but couldn't let the tears come out. "I don't understand how your dad could be that way, but I know that's not what God is like. What a nightmare for you."

An expression of embarrassment on his face, Jake stood to his feet. "I didn't mean to dump all that on you, Tory. I'd better let you get on with your work. Thanks for listening."

"Anytime. I'm here if you ever need to talk."

"Thanks." Bits of baking-soda paste fell from his cheeks as he smiled. "Maybe I'll take you up on that sometime." He walked over to Barney and patted him affectionately on the shoulder. "And thanks, Barney, for one of the more memorable experiences of my life."

Jake turned to leave, then stopped. "Oh, I almost forgot. Rob wanted me to ask you if you could go for a trail ride with him this evening after supper. He wants to talk to you about something."

Tory nodded. "I'll see him today, too, but tell him yes. Tonight's great. Thanks."

She watched him trudge back across the archery range toward camp. In her mind she tried to picture what it must be like to survive from day to day with the heavy load of pain he carried. Until now she had always thought of him as being careless and flippant about life. Rob had seemed to be the only one who understood and continued to believe in Jake.

I'm sorry, Father, Tory prayed silently. *Forgive me for my unaccepting attitude. I judged Jake. But You knew all along that he's really hurting.*

Barney snorted and headed for the barn, turning his head slightly to the side to keep from stepping on the trailing reins. With a laugh Tory ran to catch up with him.

"OK, OK," she said, grabbing his reins and trotting along beside him. "You're right. It's time for you and everyone else to get unsaddled. You're ready for a good roll in the dirt, aren't you?"

As she led Barney into the barn, Tory passed Blackberry's stall. She could see untouched grain in the young mare's feed bin. The saddle and bridle still hung over the stall door. Obviously the horse refused to come near them, even if it meant missing a meal.

Tory thought about her trail ride with Rob tonight. A sense of loss washed over her as she realized she had no horse of her own to ride. Mayonnaise belonged to Allie now. And Blackberry might never be trail horse material. She knew she could choose any of the other horses for the ride, but it wouldn't be the same.

Thoughts of the day's events—the wild trail ride, Jake's stings and his revelation of his home life, LeAnne's illness, her frustration with Blackberry—all together they threatened to overwhelm her. It would be good to talk things over with Rob.

She grabbed a currycomb from the tack room as she led Barney to his stall. Flipping the stirrup up over the seat of the saddle, she loosened the cinch strap and pulled the saddle from the horse's back. The saddle blanket reeked of horse sweat. Tory turned it upside down over the top of the stall door to let it air out.

In smooth, sweeping motions, she brushed Barney's pure white coat. His pink skin showed through in places where the hair grew thinner. He stood perfectly still and relaxed, enjoying the brush down. His lower lip hung loose.

"You know, Barney," she said, playfully tweaking the albino's floppy lower lip, "you are actually a fine horse, even if everyone does think you're a clod." She realized as she said it, how close she'd come to not even giving him a chance to prove what he could do today. If any other horse had been available, she'd never have chosen him.

Then Tory thought of her first reaction to Allie and how wrong she'd been about her, too. Sure, Allie had problems, but she'd almost let her annoyance with the girl keep her from seeing the real person inside.

Tory scratched Barney's nose affectionately as she turned to leave the stall. She pushed the door open and almost collided with Brian in the breezeway.

"Oh, there you are," he said. "I've been looking for you. I got word from Mike about LeAnne. I'm afraid it's pretty bad news."

CHAPTER SEVEN

What is it?" Tory felt a stab of fear as she saw the panic in Brian's eyes. "What's wrong with LeAnne?"

He shook his head. "It's a growth in her abdomen, at least the size of a grapefruit. They don't know if it's cancer but as fast as it's growing, the likelihood is high. She's supposed to come home for a few weeks to gain strength, then go back for surgery."

Tory sank down onto the sandy floor of the breezeway.

"No! Not LeAnne." How could this possibly be happening? Just two years before one of her friend's mother had been diagnosed with an abdominal tumor. Within a year the woman died.

Brian sat down beside her, leaning his back against the rough wood planks of the outside of Barney's stall. "Mike's pretty shook up. He'll need our support. What do you say we get the stable spotless before they return this afternoon?" Standing, he offered Tory a hand.

She grasped it, allowing him to help her to her feet. "I can't think of any better way to work off steam than to muck out stalls."

I wonder how many stalls Mike will need to muck out before this is all over, she thought.

Barney's saddle still hung on his stall door. Tory noticed several others that hadn't been returned to the tack room. She could hear Allie down in the end stall, talking to one of the horses as she brushed him down.

"Does Allie know yet?"

"No." Brian grabbed Barney's saddle and hoisted it onto his shoulder. "You can tell her if you want to."

Taking a deep breath, she headed down the corridor toward the end stall. She wasn't sure how Allie would take the news, knowing that the girl had been friends with Mike and LeAnne for years. The couple had become almost like second parents to her.

"Mayonnaise, you and I are going to have a great time this summer," Tory could hear Allie saying. "You're the best horse in the world."

Tory swallowed hard, a lump growing in her throat. She knew Mike was right in giving the horse to the girl, but it hurt to see someone else training and spending time with him. Then she cleared her throat to let Allie know she was approaching the stall, to save the girl the embarrassment of being caught carrying on a private conversation with her horse.

Allie smiled as she entered the stall.

"Looks great, doesn't he?" The girl pointed to his mane and tail, each carefully braided.

"He does look great," Tory replied, smiling back. "You've really put a lot of time into that."

As Tory ran her hand along Mayonnaise's crest and fingered the tiny braids, she marveled at Allie's patience.

"I have something to tell you," she said finally. "It's LeAnne. She's really sick. They've found a large growth in her abdomen, and she'll have to have surgery. Mike is bringing her home this afternoon. Brian thought we should get the stable cleaned up for him so he won't have any more to worry about than he already has. What do you think?"

The red-haired girl pushed her thick glasses up on her nose and gulped. "Is LeAnne going to die? Does that growth mean she has cancer?"

Tory shook her head. "We don't know yet."

"I can't believe this." Tears filled her eyes and spilled down her cheeks. "LeAnne is so young. She doesn't deserve this."

"I know. No one does. It's pretty hard to understand." She put her arm around the girl and hugged her. "I guess we're all in this together. We'll have to really come through for Mike."

Wiping her eyes, Allie nodded. "What do you want me to do?"

"For starters, let's get all this tack put away and clean this barn until it squeaks." Tory swung the stall door open for her. "After you, my dear."

The afternoon sped by. Tory cleaned stalls, shoveling manure from each one and leveling the sand floor with a rake. Her back ached and blisters formed even with the heavy work gloves she wore to protect her hands. Allie cleaned and organized the tack room. Brian pushed load after wheelbarrow load of manure to the compost pile.

The last stall to be cleaned was Blackberry's. Tory stood at its door, thinking about the bruise on her shin from the horse's sharp hoof. Did she dare enter the stall?

"Well, girl," she said finally, grasping the shovel firmly in one hand and pushing the stall door open, "I guess you and I need to come to some kind of an understanding here."

As she slipped inside and closed the door behind her, her heart pounded. Blackberry crouched in the corner of the stall like a wild deer ready to spring away. Tory murmured comforting words to the frightened little mare, keeping up a steady stream of soothing sound. When she ran out of things to say, she recited poetry and the words to old hymns.

While she talked, Tory cautiously slid the shovel over the stall floor, scraping up manure. With each full load, she opened the door and dumped the shovelful into the wheelbarrow parked just outside. She never turned her back on Blackberry or made any sudden movements.

Gradually, the mare stopped trembling and stood quietly. She flicked her delicate ears in Tory's direction, listening to the sound of her voice.

"Hey, little one," Tory said, pleased that the mare seemed to be accepting her presence, "you just might learn to trust me yet."

The crunching sound of car tires came from the road leading past the stable. Then she heard Brian yell out a greeting from the lower pasture where he and Allie had taken some of the horses and guessed that Mike and LeAnne were home. Backing slowly out of Blackberry's stall, she latched the door quietly.

"See you later, girl," she whispered over the door to the little roan. Blackberry tossed her head and snorted.

Tory reached the bungalow just as Mike helped LeAnne from the car. The woman's face still looked pale. She held her stomach as if she were about to throw up. When she saw Tory, she smiled weakly.

"Some people will do anything for a little attention, won't they?" She tried to laugh at her own joke.

Tory hurried to LeAnne's side and helped Mike support her as she walked into the house.

"Right here will be fine," the woman said, pointing to the couch. A soft cotton quilt was spread over the couch. LeAnne sank down onto it, exhaustion lining her face. She closed her eyes with a deep sigh. Mike pulled the quilt over LeAnne's feet and gestured for Tory to follow him outside. As he passed a huge ceramic piggy bank in the entryway, he reached into his pocket, pulled out a small handful of pennies, and dropped them into the container.

"I always save my change," he whispered to her. "We've been working on filling this bank up for at least a couple years now. Never know when something really important will come up. Of course, to get the money out we'll have to break it. But that's OK."

Tory's eyes widened in amazement. "I've never seen a bank so big. It must hold several gallons." She kept her voice low to keep from disturbing LeAnne.

Once outside, Mike spoke in more normal tones, but Tory could hear the strain in his usually cheerful voice. "How's Jake, Tory? LeAnne was too sick on the way into town to tell me. Did all the riders make it back safely?"

"They're fine. Everyone's OK. And the barn is all cleaned up."

She led him back to the barn to show him all the work Allie, Brian, and she had done. Mike grinned broadly when he saw the stable area.

"All right. You guys are just all right." Tears glistened in the corners of his eyes.

Just then Brian and Allie jogged into the barn, panting from the exertion of running across the pasture in the hot sun. Allie pushed her thick glasses back up onto the bridge of her nose.

"So, how's LeAnne?" Brian asked, mopping the perspiration from his forehead with a blue bandanna.

Mike shrugged helplessly. "We don't know. The doctor doesn't know. It's in God's hands. We'll just have to pray that the surgery goes well and that it's not cancer."

Brian grabbed Mike's hand and reached out for Tory's. "Let's form a circle and pray for LeAnne right now. He loves her even more than we do."

Tory took his and Allie's hand as she bowed her head. She tried to imagine how frightened Mike and LeAnne must be right now. The disappointment over losing the chance to adopt a new baby seemed insignificant compared to this life-threatening situation.

"Father," Brian prayed, "we know You love us. We

know that everything You allow to happen to us will, in the end, be just what we would choose if we could see things from Your viewpoint. You have promised that if we put You first, all things that affect us will work together for good.

"We choose to do that now. We choose to thank You even for the things we don't understand. We lift LeAnne up to You and ask for Your protection and healing for her. We praise You for the circumstances just as they are, because we know they're in Your hands. In Jesus' name, Amen."

Tory felt warm tears brimming in her eyes as she listened to Brian's prayer. When she opened her eyes, she saw Mike and Allie wiping their eyes too.

"Well, gang," Mike said, "I'd say, 'let's get to work,' but it looks like you have it all done. How about 'let's do some planning for our summer skits'? LeAnne should be fine for a while. What she needs most right now is a nap."

Brian dragged four large feed buckets from the tack room and set them upside down in a circle. He smiled at Allie and Tory, motioning to the buckets. "Your seats, ladies."

Tory took her place on a bright green bucket next to Allie's red one.

Mike pulled a piece of notebook paper from his pocket and unwadded it. "I've got some notes here that I took at my last meeting with Elder Miller and the head of each department here at camp." He peered closely at the paper, trying to decipher his own writing. Tory laughed as she watched him. The samples of his handwriting that she'd seen resembled chicken scratchings.

"The plan this year is to have a big reenactment of the life of Christ from His birth to His resurrection. Each area will be responsible for one major event in His life. The waterfront staff will act out His baptism, the kitchen staff will do the miracle of feeding the 5,000, maintenance will recreate the crucifixion, and we, since we have a stable and animals, will reenact His birth."

Tory leaned forward, almost tipping her bucket over in her excitement. "Perfect. We can make a manger and set it up in one of the stalls. Merrilegs is small enough to be in the scene without crowding anyone out."

"You and Brian have to be Joseph and Mary," Allie told her. "Your long dark hair is ideal for the part."

Brian nodded in agreement. "And you, Allie, would make a great angel Gabriel."

The girl blushed to the roots of her bright-red hair, but didn't protest.

"You know," Tory said thoughtfully, "we should make this skit different than most scenes about Jesus' birth. I think we should show how painful it was for Mary to have no one believe her when she told them that she was pregnant and God was the Father of her baby."

"And how hard it was on Joseph," Brian added. "Until the angel spoke to him, he wasn't sure what to believe."

Mike chuckled. "I'll be Mary's father. I'll really give it to her for getting into so much trouble, then making up a big story to cover it up."

"We'll have the best nativity scene ever produced," Allie announced, clapping her hands.

Mike glanced at his watch, then whistled in surprise. "Would you look at that? Supper time already." He stood up and carried his bucket back to the tack room. "You guys go on to the cafeteria, I'm going back to the house to check on LeAnne."

Tory replaced her bucket and started slowly walking down the breezeway and out through the hitching area to the sandy road that led to the cafeteria. Brian and Allie soon caught up with her.

"I want to do some thinking," Tory said. "Don't wait for me. I'll be there when I get there."

Allie looked at her quizzically. "Are you sure? Are you OK?"

"I'm fine, thanks. I just need to think through some of the stuff that happened today."

"OK," Brian grinned, "we'll let you. Come on, Allie. It's corn on the cob and tomato sandwiches tonight. I don't want to miss it."

Tory watched them hurry down the road to the cafeteria. It was hard to believe so much had happened in just one day. She thought about skipping supper and going back to her cabin to crawl into her bunk for a nap. Then she remembered.

Tonight is my trail ride with Rob.

In all the excitement over LeAnne and planning the nativity scene, she'd completely forgotten. Then she smiled to herself.

Father, your timing is always impeccable. Rob is the perfect person to talk to about everything that's going on with LeAnne and Jake.

❋ ❋ ❋

Tory slipped her riding boots and socks off and walked in the soft warm sand. The sun, though far from setting, hung too low in the western sky to keep the sand uncomfortably hot. As she strolled along she thought of Rob's promise to share with her the radical changes that had taken place in his life in the last year. *Maybe he'll tell me his story tonight.*

Suddenly not tired at all, she picked up her pace.

CHAPTER
EIGHT

The sun hung low in the west by the time Tory led Toby and Midnight to the hitching rail. When she saw Rob hurrying across the archery range toward the stable, trying to keep his hat on his head as he ran, she sat down in the sand to wait for him.

Tory loved riding the trails at dusk when the clouds glowed pink against a darkening sky and long shadows played tricks on her eyes. The horses, seeming to sense her mood, perked up their ears and pawed the ground, eager to be on their way.

"Did you give up on me?" Rob asked when he reached the hitching area.

Tory shook her head and smiled. "Nope, I figured someone waylaid you and you'd be here when you got here." She tossed Toby's reins to Rob. "This is my favorite time to ride anyway."

"Good." Rob sighed with relief. "Let's go!"

Tory walked Midnight in a small circle then tugged on his cinch strap to tighten it. In one smooth movement, she slipped the toe of her boot into the stirrup and swung into the saddle. The coal-black gelding stood quietly, waiting for commands.

"You are an amazing critter, Midnight," she told him, squeezing her heels into the horse's sides and guiding him out onto the trail. She glanced back to see how Rob fared with Toby.

Rob held the reins at perfect tension—not so loose as to give the horse too much control over the situation, but not tight enough to hurt his mouth. She watched him use leg signals to communicate with Toby. The horse seemed to respond to his rider's quiet confidence in the saddle by eagerly obeying every command.

"Let's take the river trail," Tory suggested as he trotted Toby up beside Midnight. "It's a great loop. We'll just avoid the new section of trail where the yellow jackets live."

"You're the trail boss. I'm with you," he replied, tipping his hat.

A soft breeze sprang up, rustling the leaves of the scrub-oak trees beside the airstrip trail. The horses stepped out eagerly, invigorated by the cooler air and the prospects of following the trails at their own pace, unhindered by the usual long, slow line of riders. Tory felt Midnight's body tremble with the urge to run. She glanced over at Rob and grinned as she leaned forward in the saddle.

"Let's let 'em go all out."

Rob nodded and gave Toby his head. Instantly, both horses leaped from a walk to a gallop, racing neck-and-neck down the airstrip. Tory clung to Midnight's back, closing her eyes to protect them from his snapping mane. She heard Rob let out a war whoop above the thunder of Toby's hooves.

We must be almost to the river trail, Tory thought, her eyes still shut tight, her body hugging Midnight's neck. *Midnight knows the trail. I'm sure he'll slow down when we get there.*

Suddenly, without changing his pace at all, Midnight turned sharply to the left. Tory felt herself soaring through the air. She hit the ground with a sickening thud, then lay unable to move. When she tried to breathe, she couldn't draw any air into her burning lungs. Her chest ached.

"Are you OK?"

Tory opened her eyes to see Rob leaning over her, a stricken look on his face. He held Toby's reins in one hand and Midnight's in the other. Managing to nod, she took a deep breath, relieved that she could do it.

"Can you move everything? Did you hit your head? How does your back feel?" Rob knelt on the ground beside her and started methodically checking her arms and legs for any sign of broken bones.

Slowly Tory sat up. "I'm OK. I just got the breath knocked out of me. Let's go before it gets too dark to ride along the river." Rob reached out a hand and helped her to her feet, then gave her Midnight's reins.

"Are you sure you feel like riding? That was a nasty spill. Midnight turned onto the river trail without so much as a change in leads." Rob shook his head. "I looked up and all I saw were those boots of yours flying through the air."

Tory laughed. "I wish it *had* been just my boots. I'm afraid the rest of me is going to be pretty sore." She climbed back up onto Midnight's back. "Let's just take it easy for a while."

Loosening Midnight's reins, Tory let him pick his way along the river trail at his own pace. Rob and Toby kept pace close behind, the latter carefully avoiding crowding Midnight's backside. As a veteran trail horse, he knew better than to push his luck by getting within range of those powerful hindquarters.

Tory twisted around in the saddle and smiled at the sight of Rob slouched casually in the saddle, his hat pulled low over his eyes. He looked for all the world like a cowboy from the Australian outback on his Brumby.

"Hey, Rob, you mentioned earlier that you'd tell me what happened to you that changed your life so much. Do you feel like talking about it?"

Rob pushed his hat back from his forehead. Tory

could see the twinkle in his brown eyes even in the gathering darkness.

"My favorite story to tell," he said, chuckling. The trail widened as it approached the Indian village and Rob pulled Toby up close beside Midnight.

"I grew up with an alcoholic father. Not a pretty picture because he got awfully mean when he was drunk. I hated him for what he did to our family."

Tory watched his face as he talked. Although she could hear the pain in his voice, it was unlike the hatred she'd seen in Jake's face earlier that afternoon.

"I couldn't bring my friends home," Rob continued. "I never knew what kind of condition we'd find my dad in. I made excuses for him, for our family. Everyone else seemed so happy. I watched other families doing things together and wondered why my family had to be so messed up. It didn't seem fair.

"It hurt so bad, I started taking drugs to numb the pain. Sometimes I think I did it to punish God for letting my family be such a disaster. Of course, I didn't think of it that way at the time. I just didn't care.

"When I came to camp last summer as a counselor, I had to leave the drugs behind. I knew I couldn't smoke pot here or do any of the other stuff I was doing. I'm not sure why I even agreed to come. I guess God was tugging on my heart even then.

"Watching all of you guys being so happy and at peace with yourselves made me feel even worse. I left here at the end of the summer feeling like someone had taken a bulldozer to my insides. I got so depressed I decided to go back to the drugs and give up on this 'religion' thing altogether."

Rob winced at the memory. Then he grinned at her.

"But God wasn't about to let me go so easily. One day I sat at my parents' house looking out the picture window at the fall flowers in my mom's garden. The sky was a brilliant blue and the lawn lush and green. I planned to meet a friend in town to score some drugs.

"Suddenly a voice spoke to me. It didn't speak out loud, like someone in the room with me. It was in my head. But I knew it had nothing to do with my own thoughts because they were all wrapped up in plans for partying.

"The voice said, 'Everything good in life comes from Me. Without Me, there is no meaning in anything. Would you like to see what life without My presence is like?'

"As I looked out that window, suddenly everything I saw became totally flat. The sky was still blue. The flowers were still red, orange, and white. The grass was still green. But the colors had no meaning, no vibrancy, no life. All I could see and feel was an incredibly deep sense of emptiness like nothing I'd ever experienced before.

"Then, as suddenly as it began, the emptiness vanished. The life returned to everything and I could feel again.

"'OK, Father,' I prayed. 'I hear you. I can't live apart from you. Here's my life, as messed up as it is. Take it. I won't hold anything back.'"

The boy shook his head in wonder.

"That's when the *real* miracle started. God started pouring out incredible blessings. Studying the Bible became my passion. All those things that seemed so confusing to me before, now are becoming clearer and clearer. I used to hate reading Psalms. The psalms seemed boring and made no sense. Now I love them. They say just what I want to say to God. I'm beginning to understand just a little of how much Jesus sacrificed for me. It's amazing."

Tory took a deep breath.

"Your story gives me goosebumps, Rob," she said quietly. "Thanks for sharing it with me."

Rob shifted his weight in the saddle as if realizing for

the first time since he had started talking that he was still on horseback.

"Thank *you* for listening. It means a lot to me. I just wish Jake could find the healing I've found."

She nodded solemnly. "We'll have to just keep praying for him." Then she went on to relate the day's events to Rob, including Jake's conversation with her after the trail ride.

Rob nodded in understanding. "I'm glad he opened up to you, too. It's good to know someone else will be praying for him who understands what he's been through."

The tepees of the Indian village loomed up ahead. Tory could see their giant crossed lodgepoles against the purple sky. A jay screamed, hopping from branch to branch beside the trail.

"Oh, go to bed," she said to the obnoxious bird. "We're not taking over your territory."

Rob laughed. "Maybe we should. This looks like a great place to settle in. Comfortable tepees to live in, a fire pit all ready for a roaring campfire . . ."

"I wish life could be that simple," she replied with a sigh. "Sometimes I think I was born 200 years too late. Everything seems so complex now. It's overwhelming."

He rubbed his chin thoughtfully. "Yeah, I feel pretty overwhelmed sometimes, too. The exciting part about it, though, is that the things that are so overwhelming and scary are all signs that Jesus is coming soon. Just think, *we're* the ones that will get to see Him come!"

Tory tried to imagine what the Second Advent would be like. She pictured herself on Mayonnaise riding along a mountain trail when that small dark cloud appeared in the east. The cloud grew bigger and bigger, like a huge flower opening up in the sky. Soon the whole sky was filled with bright light. As her eyes adjusted, she could see thousands of shining beings, all of them on gorgeous white horses, galloping through the air toward her. Jesus sat on a breathtakingly beautiful horse with eyes like fire and a flowing mane that resembled spun crystal.

As Jesus held out His hand to her, she could see a scar in His palm. He spoke her name and she felt Mayonnaise's feet leave the ground, rising up and up over the mountain top toward the radiant throng of riders.

Rob's voice broke through her reverie.

"Tory, did you hear anything I said?"

He pulled his horse up close beside Midnight and waved his hand in front of her eyes as if checking for consciousness.

"Uh, no. Sorry." She smiled self-consciously. "I was daydreaming." She looked around. By now they were in the Indian camp circling the fire pit.

"It's too late for daydreaming," Rob said, reining Toby back toward the trail. "Daytime is officially gone. That's what I was just telling you. I think we should head back the way we came before it's too dark to see and one of the horses trips on something."

Tory followed his lead, urging Midnight back onto the trail behind Toby. As she rode along, she gazed up into the night. A smattering of stars freckled the dark sky.

Angel kisses, Tory mused, thinking of her grandmother's teasing about her own freckles. Crickets chirped insistently from their hiding places beside the trail. An owl, out for an early evening hunting expedition, swooped low overhead. Tory felt his presence more than she heard it. His giant wings made an almost inaudible whoosh as he flew in search of prey.

I'm glad I'm not a mouse or a rabbit in the scrub tonight. Tory shuddered at the thought. Although she knew the owl had to eat, still there was something ominous about his silent approach and deadly accuracy. She thought about LeAnne and how frightened she must be right now, wondering what the future held for her, just as a rabbit trembles in the thicket while the owl passes overhead, ready to pounce.

Father, give her peace, Tory prayed. *And show me what I can do to help her.*

CHAPTER NINE

Blackberry stirred nervously in her stall as Tory approached. It had been days since she had even attempted to work with the little mare. Concerns over LeAnne's health, and preparation for the arrival of the first batch of campers, had occupied her every waking moment.

"It's OK, girl," she said soothingly. "You'll just have to get used to me. We've got a lot of adventures ahead of us, you and me."

Snorting, Blackberry shied away from her as she slipped into the stall. Tory held a halter and lead rope behind her back in one hand, and a carrot in the other. Edging toward the mare's head and shoulders and avoiding the lightning-swift hind feet, she kept up a constant stream of conversation.

Gradually Blackberry stopped trembling and stood in one place, allowing Tory to touch her. The girl held the carrot close to the little mare's delicate nostrils. Carefully Blackberry sniffed it, then opened her mouth to nibble it.

"All right," Tory said, moving in closer to the horse's shoulder. She ran her hand along Blackberry's withers and across her back, then up the arch of her crest to her ears. "I know you're frightened. I'm a little nervous myself because you're bigger than me, and I'm not too thrilled about getting stamped. So let's be nice to each other, OK?".

Smoothly Tory pulled the halter from behind her back. Before Blackberry could shy away from it, she slipped it over her nose and ears and buckled it under the throat. The mare jerked her head up and rolled her eyes in fear. When Tory snapped the lead shank onto the halter, Blackberry exploded. Instantly Tory ducked into the corner of the stall as the terrified horse reared straight up, her forelegs pawing the air.

"Whoa, girl. Easy. Steady there." Tory pulled on the lead rope, applying gentle, constant pressure. Blackberry dropped back down but stood with every muscle taut and her legs bunched under her, ready to jump again at the least provocation.

Once again Tory approached her, soothing the mare with her voice.

"Somebody sure must have treated you badly somewhere along the line. Did they tie you up and hit you?"

When she reached out to touch Blackberry's neck, the mare flinched and jerked away. Tory stepped closer, talking softly all the while. Finally, she stood next to the horse, smoothing Blackberry's dark tousled mane and stroking her neck gently.

"That wasn't so bad, was it?" Tory stood silently for several minutes, allowing the horse time to become accustomed to her touch, reassuring her that she had no intention of hurting her. Then she quietly opened the stall door.

"Come on, girl. Time for the next lesson in how to be a well-mannered horse." She tugged gently on the lead rope, encouraging Blackberry to follow her. "I know you can do this. Mike led you in here in the first place."

Tossing her head, Blackberry stepped hesitantly forward. Immediately Tory pulled the lead rope taut, then took another step. The mare followed. Tory led her down the corridor and into the bright sunshine.

When the horse stepped out into the sunlight, Tory

stared in amazement at her. The thousands of silver hairs sprinkled through her dark-blue coat from her muzzle to her hocks caught the sun and shimmered like the northern lights.

Allie stood by the corral, brushing Merrilegs down. She whistled softly when she saw the mare. "What a beauty she is. Just look at that coat. I've never seen such gorgeous coloring."

Tory led Blackberry to the hitching rail and tied the lead shank to the pole.

"Say a prayer for me, Allie," she said, grimly. "I'm going to try to ride her today."

The red-haired girl's eyes widened in surprise, but she said nothing. Tory left Blackberry tied to the rail and walked back into the barn to get her saddle from the tack room. On the way back, the saddle slung over her shoulder, she felt her knees weakening. Her stomach lurched and her heart pounded.

Can I do this? Tory thought of stories she'd heard of untameable horses that threw their riders to the ground, then turned around and stamped them. Taking a deep breath, she pushed the fear from her mind. *Mike believes I can do this or he wouldn't have asked me to.*

With a grunt, Tory heaved the heavy saddle over the hitching rail. She held the saddle blanket in her right hand and approached Blackberry with it, keeping it low to avoid any quick movements that might frighten the mare unnecessarily. Touching the blanket to Blackberry's skin, she slid it slowly over the horse's body.

At first Blackberry lurched and jerked at the lead rope, her eyes wild and her muscles tense. But as Tory continued rubbing the blanket on Blackberry's back, neck, legs, and hind quarters, the little horse calmed down.

"See there? I told you it wouldn't be so bad," Tory crooned. She positioned the saddle blanket in the center of Blackberry's back, then reached for the saddle. The leather squeaked as she flipped it in place and the mare shot straight up as if she'd been blown from a cannon. The saddle flew one direction and the saddle blanket the other. Blackberry shook herself like a wet dog, obviously glad to be rid of both of them.

Allie laughed out loud, then clapped her hand over her mouth. "I'm sorry, Tory. I didn't mean to laugh at you."

The stricken look in the girl's eyes startled Tory.

"It's OK," she said, grinning. "Sometimes we have to laugh to keep from crying." Picking the saddle blanket out of the sand, she brushed it off.

"Blackberry old girl, you may as well give in now and save us both a lot of trouble, because sooner or later I'm going to win." She placed the blanket back on the mare's back.

Blackberry stood quietly while Tory replaced the saddle, reaching under the horse's belly to pull the cinch strap tight. She got the cinch partially tightened when the little mare exploded again. Tory held her breath while Blackberry pitched and crow-hopped, hoping the saddle would stay in place. When the mare finally came to a stop, Tory deftly tightened the cinch the rest of the way and secured it.

"Whew!" She stepped back and leaned against the hitching rail. "That was a job."

Allie gave her the thumbs-up signal. "Just a minute, and I'll put Merrilegs back in his stall. I'll hold Blackberry for you while you get on. I have a hunch it will take both of us."

Tory walked Blackberry around the sandy area along the hitching rail. The saddle squeaked softly with each step. Blackberry kept one ear directed back toward it and the other toward Tory.

Emerging from the barn, Allie approached Blackberry cautiously. The mare's bridle hung over her shoulder. She took the mare's lead rope from Tory and handed her the bridle.

"I don't know if Blackberry has ever even had a bit in her mouth," Tory said. "Nor have I any idea how she'll react. But I guess we're about to find out."

Tory held the bridle by the bit in her left hand, making sure the headstall of the bridle was straight, without twists or kinks. She stood facing forward beside Blackberry's head and curled her right arm under the mare's jaw and up over her nose. This allowed her to use her body weight as an anchor to hold Blackberry's head down. Then she slipped the bit quickly into the horse's mouth, flipping the bridle's headstall up over her ears and fastening the throatlatch strap before the mare had time to react.

"Wow," Allie breathed. "That had to be some kind of world record. How'd you do that so fast?"

Tory laughed. "Lots of practice and the threat of bodily harm. Great combination."

Blackberry champed at the bit, appearing more fascinated than frightened at the cold foreign object in her mouth. Tory motioned to Allie to hold the lead rope tight. She flipped the reins over Blackberry's head so she could hold them from the back and edged close to the mare's side.

"Here goes." Tory gritted her teeth, slipping the toe of her boot into the stirrup and swinging quickly into the saddle. Once mounted, she kicked her toe free to avoid having her foot caught in the stirrup should she be thrown off.

Allie held the lead rope while Tory settled herself in the saddle.

"OK. Unsnap it. I'm ready."

Removing the lead rope, the red-headed girl stepped back. "You're on your own, Tory. Try not to get killed."

Blackberry stood stock-still, her legs planted firmly and her sides heaving, for what seemed like eternity. Tory sat, tense, bracing herself mentally for the showdown she knew was coming, but trying to keep her body limber enough to take the jolts without breaking something.

"Come on, girl," she said softly. "Let's get on with this. Do what you're going to do." She squeezed the mare's sides with her legs.

Suddenly Blackberry leaped straight up in the air, landing with her head down between her legs. The mare crow-hopped across the barn lot, hitting the ground like a jackhammer with each jump. They whirled in circles until Tory's head spun. Tory clung to the saddle horn to maintain her balance. Every jerk of Blackberry's body sent shock waves up her spine.

I don't know how much more of this I can take, she thought. *But I think it would hurt worse to bail off.*

Gradually, Blackberry's bucking lost its fury. A few more half-hearted crowhops and her gait smoothed into an easy canter. Tory breathed a sigh of relief.

Allie hurried over to help her dismount. Grinning feebly, Tory handed her the reins. "Well, round one is over and I'm still conscious. What do you think?"

The other girl shook her head. "Pretty amazing. I don't think I've ever seen a horse put up that stiff a fight. She's got spunk, all right." She reached out a hand to help Tory down.

Tory's legs felt like cornmeal mush as she tried to walk to the hitching rail. She wobbled so badly that she finally had to sit down on the ground. Just then she looked up to see Mike trotting across the field from his house.

"Hey, that was a pretty impressive piece of bronco riding you did there young'un," he said when he reached the hitching area. "I was watching you from my window. You'll have that mare broke in three shakes of a monkey's tail."

Blackberry stood, feet apart and head down, by the rail. White foam covered her chest and sweat dripped from her belly. Mike loosened the cinch and pulled the saddle from her back, flipping the saddle blanket upside down over the hitching rail to dry out.

"Better walk her some," he said to Allie. "She's pretty hot."

Tory watched her pull Blackberry's bridle off and snap the lead shank back onto the halter. The mare didn't protest when Allie coaxed her into walking out into the field beyond the barn lot. It seemed that the last of her resistance, for today at least, had drained out in those last few crowhops.

Mike sat down beside Tory. "Allie's doing a lot better, don't you think?" he said, watching the girl's retreating figure. "She's had a hard row to hoe. Working with the horses is making a big difference in how she feels about herself. She kinda reminds me of Blackberry, spooked by life and just needing some love and patience to bring out the best in her."

Nodding, Tory listened as Mike continued.

"LeAnne and I want to do something more to help her. We're thinking about buying contact lenses for her so she doesn't have to wear those heavy glasses."

Tory smiled to herself. It was just like Mike and LeAnne to come up with something like that. "I think it'd be great, Mike. When are you going to do it?"

Mike dug little furrows in the sand with his index finger. "I don't know. It should be sometime special. I'll have to think about it. In the meantime, I have something for *you* to think about. Are you recovered enough yet?"

"Sure," she said, curious. "What's up?"

He cleared his throat.

"Well, week after next is blind camp, and we're several counselors short this year. Elder Miller just asked me if you would be willing to fill in. We could get by here at the stable just for that week. How about it?"

Tory gulped. *Blind camp?* She'd never been around a

blind person before, much less been responsible for a cabin full of blind children day and night for a whole week.

Father, is this what you want me to do? She felt that old familiar tug at her heart, compelling her to say yes.

"OK," she said, "I'll do it."

"Good. I'll tell Elder Miller. It'll be an experience to tell your grandchildren about, believe me."

She laughed. "Oh, I believe you. The way this summer's going, I think I could write a whole book about it."

CHAPTER TEN

An old yellow bus rounded the curve and chugged through the camp's entrance gate. It hissed to a stop right in front of the patch of grass where Tory sat waiting.

Through the windows she could see rows and rows of children's faces. But these kids didn't hang out the windows yelling at passersby. They sat quietly in their seats, waiting to be told it was safe to step off the bus.

All week, since Mike had asked her to be a blind camp counselor, Tory had been gearing up for the experience. She watched the blind children filing down the steps of the bus, heads tilted to hear the least sound, and realized that nothing could have prepared her for this.

Children are supposed to run and play, climb trees, and ride horses. How can these children experience life without their eyes? Tory felt a lump rising up in her throat. It just seemed all wrong.

Several staff members guided the children through the registration line. Tory hurried to her place at the end of the line to receive her campers as they registered.

A tiny girl clutching a rag doll moved through the line quickly. Tory noticed the girl's total absence of color. Her thick, waist-length hair and her skin were pure white. Only her eyes shone pink in the sunlight.

Trying not to stare, Tory decided that the little girl's coloring looked just like Barney's.

"Hi, I'm Dianna," the child said, planting herself directly in front of Tory. "I'm an albino, and if you're Tory, I'm in your cabin."

"Uh, yes. I'm Tory. But how did you know?"

Dianna smiled and pointed at the registration table. "A lady at that table told me. Besides, I can see a little. More than most of the kids. Some of 'em can't see at *all*."

"Well, Dianna," Tory said, grateful that at least one of her campers was not totally blind, "you'll have to be my assistant and help me with the kids who can't see as well as you can."

As each of the girls assigned to Tory's cabin filed through registration, Dianna herded them into a line of her own. Within minutes, she'd gleaned important basic information from each one. Tory stood by the table, still leafing through the stack of profiles the registrar had given her.

Dianna pulled on the sleeve of Tory's shirt. "Tory, we're all here. Do you want me to tell you about everybody?"

Still trying to match health histories with the young faces in front of her, Tory nodded. Dianna started at the head of her line. She pulled a small red-headed girl forward. Her thick glasses magnified her eyes, giving her an almost cartoon-like appearance.

"This is Judy," Dianna said as if she'd known the girl all her life. "She can see a little bit, too. But not as good as me. Her mom is a teacher."

"Hi, Judy." Tory smiled at the girl. "Welcome to Cool Springs Camp. I'm glad you're here."

One by one, Dianna introduced each of the campers. Natalie, the shy one, tall for her age and in love with her cats. Angelina, the Mexican-American, endowed with a special gift for music. Carmen, whose father owned a candy shop. Marie, the Black girl and the other albino in the group, with pure white hair and fair skin. And Bob, whose real name was Barbara but didn't want to be called that, ever.

"All right, campers," Tory said, pulling herself up to her full height to appear confident and in charge of the situation. "Let's collect our gear and march to the cabin." She turned and started toward the yellow bus where several guys were unloading the campers' gear onto the lawn. She heard snickering behind her and realized no one was following.

"Psst, Tory." Dianna stood apart from the others, one hand cupped around her mouth, the other on her hip. "Are you forgetting something? They can't follow you, they're *blind*."

As Tory stopped dead in her tracks she felt her face grow hot. Of course the girls couldn't find their way on their own. She would have to guide them everywhere they went. But how could she hold seven hands at once? Then she had an idea.

"Each of you take the hand of the person next to you. Dianna, you may be the tail of the line, and I'll be the head. This way we can stay together."

Tory took Natalie's hand and helped the others find a hand to grab until they had formed a human chain. Then Tory started walking toward the luggage. Progress was slow, with lots of stumbling, but they made it.

There's got to be a better way, Tory thought. *If the line didn't fan out so wide, they wouldn't encounter so many obstacles. Somehow, we have to figure out a way to walk in single file.*

A crew of counselors and waterfront staff waited to carry the luggage to the cabins. Rob and Jake stood by the luggage, checking labels and doling belongings out to their rightful owners. Rob's face lit up when he saw Tory.

"The Wrangler Woman!" He turned to Jake. "I've seen this girl fly. It was amazing."

Jake grinned. "I believe it. I've seen her run a horse so fast, I thought they were both going to take off."

Rob pulled a rope from the handles of a group of suitcases and duffel bags. "Here are your bags," he said to Tory. She eyed the rope lying on the ground.

"Hey, Rob, could I borrow that this week? I'll give it back when you're ready to tie the baggage back up next Sunday."

He looked puzzled but readily agreed. Tory dropped Natalie's hand. "Just a minute, girls. Stay put. I want to try something."

The soft cotton rope was perfect for what she had in mind. She tied seven large knots, each at least two feet apart, in the length of rope.

"Each of you grab a knot," she instructed her campers. "I'll hold the end of the rope, and you all follow me single-file, holding onto your knot. That way I can lead us in a straight line, avoiding things we might trip on."

The girls chattered excitedly as they found their places on the rope. Several of the waterfront staff picked up the assortment of luggage and started across camp toward the girls' cabin area.

"Which cabin?" one of the lifeguards called back over his shoulder.

"Bluebird!" the girls shouted in unison.

Tory picked up her end of the rope and cleared her throat loudly. "OK. Is everyone ready? Do you have your knot?"

The campers giggled, and each one held her knot high in the air.

"Great. Follow me, then. Forward march. On to Bluebird!"

As Tory picked her way across the lawn she was acutely aware of every tree root and hole in the ground that might cause one of the girls to stumble. She glanced back frequently, checking for signs of problems. Each of the campers clutched her knot tightly, but everyone moved across the rough ground smoothly and with confidence.

Just before she reached the cabin area, Tory turned to

make sure the girls were negotiating the rough ground without mishap. Suddenly the toe of her shoe caught on a root, pitching her forward, face first, onto the dusty trail.

"Are you all right, Tory?" several of the campers called out.

She picked herself up, brushing the dirt from her jeans. Just then she felt a tug on her sleeve and glanced down to see Marie, a mischievous grin on her face.

"Whatsa matter, Tory, can't you see where you're going? Are you blind or something?"

The rest of the group roared with laughter. Dianna doubled over in glee while Angelina and Carmen sat down in the trail, holding their stomachs as they laughed. Natalie felt her way up the rope to Tory's hand. She reached out and touched her counselor's arm.

"We aren't making fun of you," she said quietly. "Are you OK?"

Tory put her arm around Natalie's shoulder. "I'm fine. I thought it was funny, too." She watched Natalie retrace her way back down the rope to her knot.

What an incredible bunch of kids, Tory mused. *There's no self-pity here.*

Bluebird cabin rested in a grove of trees, facing six other rustic buildings just like it. A large painting of a bluebird hung beside the door. The cabin consisted of two large rooms with a tiny bathroom in between. Bunk beds lined the walls and an ancient dresser squatted in a corner of each room.

Tory wrinkled her nose at the mixed odor of mildew, old mosquito repellent, and sulfur water that permeated the cabin. A cockroach skittered across the damp cement floor and disappeared under one of the bunks.

"Wow, this is great," Bob shouted, throwing her sleeping bag onto one of the top bunks. She unrolled it and plopped her pillow at the head. Then she emptied her pockets and carefully placed a Boy Scout knife, a flashlight, and a compass on top of her pillow.

"That's a nice compass, Bob," Tory said, making plenty of noise as she moved so she wouldn't startle the girl. Bob picked the compass up and held it tightly in her hand.

"Yeah. My dad gave it to me for Christmas. He used to take me camping a lot. He was teaching me to use it when I got sick and lost my eyesight." Her voice caught and her lower lip trembled slightly. "Dad thinks I can't go camping now because I can't see. But I'm going to show him I can do anything I want to."

Tory reached out and squeezed her hand. "Your dad's lucky to have a daughter like you."

"He wanted a boy," she said, her voice tight. "A boy that could see."

The pain in the girl's voice cut Tory's heart like a knife. She sent up a silent prayer for her.

Father, I wish I could fix the hurts in this little girl's life—in all their lives. But I know I can't. Please wrap Your arms around her and let her know You love her.

Suddenly Tory realized that God *was* reaching out to Bob and the six other girls in her cabin. He was reaching out to them through her.

Here I am, Father. I'll be Your love with skin on. Just show me how.

Angelina sat cross-legged on one of the bottom bunks. She had pushed her duffel bag under the end of her bed and lined up her shoes in a neat row beside it. Now she held a wooden flute in her hand.

Pushing a strand of coal-black hair from her eyes, the girl lifted the instrument to her mouth and began to play. The other girls stopped in their tracks and clapped in time to the lively Spanish tune.

"All right!" Tory exclaimed when Angelina finished her song. "We have a musician among us. Would you be willing to play for our worship time every night?"

Angelina smiled shyly and nodded. "I know some good God songs. My grandmother taught me. I'll be glad to play for you."

A lion roared in the camp zoo on the other side of the trees bordering the cabin area. The girls jumped, startled.

"What was that?" Natalie whispered.

Tory chuckled. "It's OK. It's not running around loose. That's old Nero, the lion. He lives in the zoo."

Natalie brightened. "Really? A lion here at camp?" She hugged a cat plush toy she'd brought from home. "Do you think I could see him, Tory? I've dreamed of seeing a real live lion for as long as I can remember."

For a moment Tory stood speechless. How could Natalie see the lion when she was blind? Then she remembered something Rob had told her in preparation for blind camp.

"To a blind person, feeling is seeing," he had said. "When the person says 'I want to see that,' he or she means, 'let me touch that so I can learn about its shape, size, and texture and form a picture of it in my mind.'"

"Maybe we will get a chance to see the lion," Tory said. "And lots of other animals, too."

Dianna snuggled close, her little arm around Tory's waist. "I can't wait to ride the horses," she said, smiling up at Tory. "When can we go?"

Tory gulped as she thought of the last staff trail ride with its frantic horses plowing into the brush to escape from the angry yellow jackets. How could she endanger the girls' lives like that?

Marie hugged Tory from the other side, locking arms with Dianna behind Tory's back. "The lady at the registration table said we can go horseback riding tomorrow."

Tory laughed. "I guess it's official then. Tomorrow it is."

CHAPTER ELEVEN

The horses stood placidly at the hitching rail as Tory and the seven girls marched across the field toward the stable, each holding tightly to her knot in the rope.

"Hey, Tory," Marie yelled, "we're getting good at walking places with this rope."

Tory had to agree that the rope made all the difference. *But we won't be able to use the rope on horseback. How in the world will they know which way to guide the horses when they can't see?*

Concern for the campers' safety tugged at her thoughts. When Mike emerged from the barn whistling Yankee Doodle, Tory felt almost irritated with him for being so cheerful. Brian led Old Henry to the hitching rail, smiling broadly when he saw Tory.

"Hi, Tory. Are you ready to take these boys on the adventure of their lives?"

All the girls except Bob stomped their feet and shouted, "We're not boys. Can't he tell a girl from a boy?"

Brian winked at Tory and walked back into the barn. As Allie stood by the rail, tightening Barney's cinch, Mike led Big Jim out of his stall and tied him to the rail close to where Tory stood. The head wrangler tightened Jim's cinch strap, then gave the Belgian one last pat before returning to the barn for another horse.

Tory leaned over and kissed Jim on the nose. "You are

truly the sweetheart of the stable," she whispered. "I wish every horse here had your heart." Big Jim nuzzled her, looking for treats.

Natalie pressed close to the huge horse. "I wish I could ride you," she said, running her hands down his neck to his massive shoulder.

Mike appeared at her side. "You can ride him. He'd be a good one for you." He reached for Natalie's hand and guided it to the stirrup. "OK. Put your left foot in here and bounce just a little to get up into the saddle. I'll help you."

Natalie followed his instructions precisely. Once in the saddle, she sat tall, her face glowing with pride. Mike leaned over to Tory and whispered, "I'd rather take blind kids on a trail ride than sighted ones any day. They listen better and do what you tell 'em!"

Then he turned to Angelina, who was next in line. "You look like a good match for Midnight. You both have dark hair and lots of style. Come on, and I'll help you up."

Tory marveled again at Mike's skill in combining campers with horses. When he put them together, something almost magical seemed to happen, bringing out the very best in both horse and rider. She stood back and watched, curious to see which animal he would choose for each of her girls.

Mike matched feisty little Dianna with Barney, red-headed Judy with Jasmine, Carmen with Merrilegs, Marie with the beautiful black and white paint, Monday, and Bob with Toby.

As Tory hurried from horse to horse helping Brian and Allie check cinches and raise or lower stirrups to adjust to each camper's height she noticed that Mike had left each of the horse's lead shanks tied to the hitching rail even though he'd given the reins to the girls.

"Now listen up, cowgirls," Mike said in a loud voice when all the campers were ready. "The information I'm about to give you could mean the difference between a great trail ride and a disaster. How many of you want to go on a great trail ride?"

"Yeah! We do!" the girls shouted in unison. Tory caught Allie's eye and grinned. Allie winked back.

"A great trail ride has rules," Mike continued. "Even the old wagon train expeditions had rules. So here they are: First, never pass the horse ahead of you or let your horse stop in the middle of the trail. Second, if your horse does run away with you for some reason, grab one rein as close to the horse's bit as possible and pull it down hard toward your foot on that side. A horse can't run very far or very fast with his head twisted around backward. Got those two?"

"Yes!" the girls chorused.

"Each of you must memorize your horse's name because two or three of you will be riding in front of each of the wranglers on their horses. When you need to turn right, your wrangler will say, 'Big Jim, right.' Or if you need to stop, it will be 'Big Jim, Whoa.' That way you will know when your horse is going to turn."

After Mike had given the general instructions, he, Tory, Allie, and Brian went from camper to camper, showing each one how to neck rein to the right or to the left and how to stop.

Dianna sat hunkered over on Barney's back as Tory approached. Tears dripped down her face, splashing on the saddle horn. Tory reached up and touched the girl's shoulder.

"Dianna. What's wrong?"

"I don't want to ride," she sobbed. "I don't like this horse. I want to go back to the cabin."

"You don't have to ride if you don't feel safe," Tory said gently. "But you can't go back to the cabin alone. I'll have to find someone to stay with you until the rest of us come back from our ride."

"But I don't want to stay with someone else. I want to be with you."

Silently Tory tried to decide how to handle the situation. Suddenly Allie appeared at her side. "Dianna, I'm Allie. Can you tell me what you're afraid of?"

The camper sniffled and wiped her face with her sleeve. "I'm afraid I'll lose my glasses," she said in a small voice. "Those guys at registration yesterday said these horses fly, especially when Tory rides them. If my horse flies with me, my glasses might fall off, then I won't be able to see at all."

Allie looked at Tory with eyebrows raised inquiringly. Tory restrained her laughter, keeping her tone serious so she wouldn't embarrass the young camper.

"Those boys were teasing me, Dianna. Horses don't fly. They usually walk very, very slowly on these trail rides. I think your glasses will be safe."

The girl sighed with relief and smiled. "OK. I'll go then."

Tory shot Allie a grateful look for her help with the situation. With a grin Allie turned to assist another camper.

Mike climbed up on Buckshot, the little bay, and rode to the end of the hitching rail. Tory and Allie quickly unsnapped the horses' lead shanks, then Allie mounted Mayonnaise as Tory led Natalie on Big Jim and Judy on Jasmine into place behind Mike. Allie fell into line behind them with Angelina on Midnight and Carmen on Merrilegs positioned behind her. Brian reined Bullet into line next. Bob on Toby, Marie on Monday, and Dianna on Barney followed.

Suddenly Tory realized she hadn't chosen a horse to ride herself.

I wish Blackberry was ready for a trail ride, she thought. Old Henry was the only horse waiting at the hitching rail for a rider.

"We have to stop meeting like this," she teased as she untied the horse and swung up into the saddle. Henry tossed his head, shaking a pesky fly from his face.

"He agreed with you," Brian said. He was twisted around in Bullet's saddle, watching her. "Did you see him nodding his head yes?"

"I have that effect on men," Tory said, flipping her hair over her shoulder. "They just can't say no to me."

His face sobered. "I'll bet that's true," he said quietly. Tory saw the same expression on Brian's face that he had the day they had talked on the airstrip. She looked away.

"Ready?" Mike called. "Let's head 'em up and move 'em out." He nudged Buckshot who started prancing sideways down the path to the airstrip. Bullet lunged and fought the bit, attempting to break out of the line and bolt, but each of the horses carrying a young camper seemed to sense the need to move carefully and behave perfectly. Even Barney cooperated with Dianna, responding to her signals without hesitation.

At the end of the airstrip, just before the trail turned a sharp left into the woods, Tory prepared each of the riders in her charge for the maneuver.

"Marie, Bob, and Dianna, listen carefully. Wait until I give you the signal. One by one, I'll tell you when to make the turn."

Tory watched for the perfect moment to have Marie follow Brian onto the river trail.

"Monday, left," she called. Marie pressed the reins over the right side of the paint's neck, guiding him to the left. "Toby, left." Bob reined Toby onto the trail in one smooth movement. "Barney, left." Dianna froze, unable to remember how to neck rein. Barney plodded along behind Toby, making the turn anyway.

"Good job, girls," Tory said, sighing with relief. She'd forgotten how well-trained the horses were.

The trail widened as the Indian village came into view. Mike led the line of riders into the Indian camp and dismounted. "Let's take a break here," he said. He tied Buckshot to a hitching rail in front of one of the tepees and motioned to the staff to help the campers do the same.

"Join hands in a line and follow me," Mike told the girls. "I want to show you something." The girls held hands and walked behind him to one of the tepees.

"Touch the sides of this tepee," he said. "See how big it is?" He led them through the camp, explaining bits of Native American history. Then he had the campers sit in a circle near the fire pit.

"Tory has a story about Indians that I'd like to have her tell you, if she will, since we're here in Indian country."

Tory nodded to him and sat down cross-legged in the circle. Allie and Brian joined the group. Tory avoided his gaze, keeping her eyes on the girls.

"Many years ago, in the days when bears and cougars roamed the wild country, and tales of Indian raids trickled back to the larger settlements in the east, a young family decided to travel west to find their fortune. It was a difficult decision to leave Grandma and Grandpa and the farm, but Ma and Pa felt it was the right thing for them to do.

"For young Toby, the hardest part was leaving his horse, Cheyenne. Pa made it clear that there wouldn't be room in the wagon for horse feed. Only the ox would be going, to pull the covered wagon over the rough roads. Pa said Toby and Josie could each choose one thing to take along. Baby Josie didn't seem to care that she could only bring one doll. Toby chose his leather pouch full of marbles.

"That pouch of marbles was Toby's pride and joy. When he couldn't find someone to play a game of marbles with him, he drew a circle in the dirt and played by himself. He loved to hold the marbles up to the sun to see them glow like fire.

"The first night of the journey, after an exhausting day plodding along under the sun, Toby grabbed his pouch of marbles and headed for a sandy spot in the clearing to play.

" 'Wait a minute there, son' Ma said, placing his wriggling baby sister in his arms. 'I need you to watch Josie while I prepare the evening meal.'

"Toby carried Baby Josie to the creek to let her splash in the cool water. Just then Jim, the wagon master's son, rode up on his spunky little bay gelding.

" 'Do you want to go exploring with me?' Jim asked. 'You can ride Ranger. He can find his way back to camp from anywhere.'

"Toby shook his head. 'I can't. I have to watch my baby sister.'

"Jim rolled his eyes in disgust. 'Baby-sitting is for girls,' he said as he rode away.

"Every evening at the end of the day's travels Toby watched baby Josie for Ma. But every day, he grew to resent it more.

" 'I wish I didn't have a sister,' he said in frustration one day. 'Then maybe I could do something I want to do for a change.'

"Ma overheard him and gave him a pained look but said nothing.

"That night around the campfire, talk turned to Indians. Several of the men had seen evidence of an Indian scouting party. Toby felt goose bumps raise up on his arms as he listened to the men talk around the crackling fire. He glanced over his shoulder into the darkness, wondering if, even now, dark eyes might be watching from the shadows.

"Just to be sure everyone was safe, Pa had the whole family sleep in the bed of the wagon that night. Toby lay awake for a long time, listening to the night birds calling and to the croaking of frogs in a nearby pond. When he finally fell asleep, he tossed fitfully, dreaming of painted faces in the moonlight and long brown arms reaching toward him.

"The early morning sun shining through a crack in the canvas awakened Toby. He groaned and rolled over. Ma had slipped out through the front of the wagon sometime earlier. Toby could smell biscuits cooking over the crackling fire. He reached over to check on baby Josie, snuggled down under a thick quilt.

" 'Josie,' Toby whispered. 'Time to get up.'

"He pulled the quilt back and saw with horror that the mound he thought was baby Josie was actually just a wad of buckskin.

" 'Ma! Pa!' he screamed. 'Baby Josie's gone!'

"Toby remembered his dream and realized that it hadn't been a dream at all. The Indians had taken the baby during the night.

"Pa and the other men gathered with the wagon master to figure out what to do. 'I'm going after her,' Pa said.

"Toby had never seen such anguish on Pa's face. The wagon master decided to send several of the men with Pa to track the Indians. The rest of the men would stay with the wagon train, just in case the Indians were setting a trap, luring the men away so they could attack the wagons.

" 'I want to go, too,' Toby said, standing as tall as he could so the others would recognize that he, too, was a man capable of tracking Indians.

" 'No,' Pa said. 'I've lost one of my children. I couldn't bear to lose you too. Besides, there's no horse for you to ride.'

"Jim, the wagon master's son, stepped forward. 'Sir, I'd be happy to let him ride Ranger.'

" 'All right, then,' Pa said. 'You may come with us. Hurry and tell your Ma, and have her gather up everything she can find to use to trade with the Indians.' Toby filled a cloth bag with the things Ma collected: a silver candlestick, several shiny spoons, some colorful beads.

"All morning long the men tracked the Indians. The trail led in a wide circle, so when the head tracker shouted that he'd spotted the Indians, Toby recognized from the surrounding rock bluffs that they really were not far from the wagon train.

"The Indians stood in a clearing, waiting for the white men. A buckskin hammock stretched between two trees beside the clearing with a baby girl in it, her face as brown as the bark on the trees and streaked with tears.

"'Pa,' Toby whispered as he pulled Ranger up beside the big-boned paint Pa had borrowed from one of the men. He pointed to the hammock. 'There's Josie over there. They painted her face!'

"His father held a finger to his lips and rode out to meet the Indians. Toby watched him pull things from Ma's cloth bag and hand them to one of the Indians. The Indian handled each one carefully, then shook his head. Finally Pa wheeled the horse around and galloped back to Toby.

"'It's not enough. They want more.' Pa's jaw looked tight the way it did when he was really upset. 'I don't want to let Josie out of my sight. Can you ride back to the wagon and get more to trade?'

"Toby nodded and headed in the direction of camp. He kicked Ranger into a full gallop, leaning low over his neck to keep from being caught on low-hanging branches. The trail, a well-worn animal highway, widened as it approached a creek. Ranger pulled to the left, although the trail veered to the right.

"'No, Ranger, it's this way,' Toby urged, certain that the camp lay at the base of the rock bluff that towered over the trees to the right. The horse tossed his head and kept trying to go to the left. Suddenly Toby remembered Jim's words: 'Ranger can find his way back to camp from anywhere.' Toby relaxed the reins and let Ranger pick his own trail. Soon the forest opened up into a clearing at the base of another rock bluff, and there, straight ahead, were the wagons.

"'Ma!' Toby shouted as he galloped Ranger into camp, 'we found Josie.'

"Ma ran from the wagon, tears streaming down her face. 'Thank God,' she sobbed. Then she looked around. 'Where is she?'

"'The Indians still have her. They want more in trade.'

"Ma climbed back into the wagon, searching frantically for items she thought the Indians would consider valuable. She found a hand mirror, a cowbell, and a small cooking pot. 'I hope this is enough,' she said, a worried look on her face.

"Toby tied Ranger to the back of the wagon and reached inside. He pulled his precious deerskin pouch from its hiding place. Ma watched as he stuffed the marbles into the cloth bag, along with the mirror, bell, and pot. Her eyes glistened with tears, but she didn't say a word.

"Once again on Ranger's back, Toby urged the horse back down the trail toward the Indian camp. Ranger seemed to sense the urgency of their mission and ran with all his heart.

"Pa's face lit up with joy and relief as Toby galloped Ranger into the clearing where the Indians stood. Toby gave the cloth bag to Pa, who handed it to the Indians. One by one the leader took the items from the bag. Not especially impressed with the mirror, the bell, or the cooking pot, the Indians grunted in surprise as the leader emptied the deerskin pouch into his hand. He held one of the clear golden marbles up and talked excitedly to the others as it caught the sun's rays.

"'Stones of fire,' the Indian said to Pa. 'Enough. You take papoose.'

"Pa hurried over to the hammock and grabbed baby Josie. He handed her to Toby while he mounted his horse. When he reached for her again, Toby shook his head.

" 'I'd like to carry her, Pa.'

"Pa nodded. 'Let's get out of here before they change their minds.'

"Toby glanced over his shoulder as he followed Pa into the woods. The Indians still stood in the clearing, examining the marbles. Toby's throat felt tight as he hugged his little sister. How could he ever have resented her?

"As the group approached camp, Ma ran to meet them. She pulled Josie from Toby's arms. Toby saw Jim, the wagon master's son, walking across camp to get his horse.

" 'Thanks, Jim,' he said as he handed Ranger's reins to Jim. 'He's a great horse. You were right about him finding camp from anywhere.'

"Jim grinned broadly. 'You're welcome to ride Ranger anytime. I'm glad he could help rescue your sister.' His face took on a wistful expression. 'I wish I had a sister. Maybe I could help you baby-sit her sometime.'

" 'Sure,' Toby said. He looked at Ma, standing there rocking Josie in her arms. 'Is that OK, Ma?'

"Ma nodded, smiling, 'I can't think of anything I'd like better than to have two strong young men protecting the baby.'

" 'Come on,' Jim said. 'Let's go exploring. Then we can play a game of marbles.'

" 'B-but, I don't have any marbles. I traded them,' Toby stammered.

"Jim pulled a small bag from his pocket. 'That's OK,' he said. 'We've got these. I brought them along from home.' Jim emptied the bag into his hand. A pile of glistening marbles caught the sunlight.

" 'Well, what are you waiting for?' The wagon

master's son shoved the marbles back in his pocket and reached out a hand to help Toby up onto Ranger, behind him.

"Toby waved at Ma as he and Jim trotted out of camp. Baby Josie lifted her chubby little hand and waved too.

"Jim laughed. 'You're sure lucky to have that sister,' he said.

"'Yes,' Toby replied. His heart felt so full of love for his sister, he thought it would burst. 'I know I am. I really am.'"

✳ ✳ ✳

The campers sat quietly for a moment when Tory finished her story.

"Oh-h-h," Natalie sighed, "I like that story. Did it really happen?"

Tory laughed. "You'll never guess who told me that story. Yes, it is true, and Baby Josie herself shared it with me."

"How could she tell you?" Judy asked shyly. "Babies can't talk."

"She wasn't a baby anymore when she told me. In fact, she was a great-grandma. Her family kept traveling by wagon train to a town in central Missouri, where they settled down to farm. Baby Josie grew up and became a school teacher. She told the story of Toby and the Indians to her children and to their children and to *their* children."

Mike stood. "Time to go. They'll send a search party out looking for us if we don't head back to camp."

"A-w-w-w," the girls groaned in unison. "We want to stay out here all day. We want to hear more stories!"

"I'll tell you stories tonight," Tory said. "Remind me at worship time and I'll tell you one they call 'The greatest story ever told.'"

"Ooh." Dianna clapped her hands in excitement. "I can't wait."

CHAPTER TWELVE

The week passed quickly, each day packed with adventure. Tory marveled at her blind campers' ability to do most anything that sighted campers were able to do.

Activities such as archery and swimming required special adaptations to accommodate the children's loss of vision. But her girls never even seemed to notice.

"Let's go to the zoo," Dianna begged on Sabbath afternoon. "This is our last day of camp. I want to say goodbye to the animals."

The other girls nodded in agreement, so Tory got out the rope. Each camper quickly took her place along it. Tory smiled as she thought of that first stumbling walk she'd taken with the girls, but how swiftly and smoothly they moved now.

The nature-center door stood ajar, allowing fresh air to circulate through the humid room. Large glass terrariums lined the walls. One section housed a variety of snakes, from deadly rattlers to huge pythons. Another section featured small furry creatures such as guinea pigs, ferrets, wood rats, raccoons, and skunks.

Tory was surprised to see Breeze, her soft black hair pulled back in a headband with a leopard-skin print, sitting on the floor in front of one of the raccoon cages.

"Hi, Tory," Breeze said warmly, jumping to her feet. "Are these your girls?"

Tory introduced her to each of the campers. She noticed with surprise how comfortably Breeze greeted the girls, reaching out to take each of their hands and repeating their names softly.

A lion roared from somewhere in the back of the zoo. Tory and Breeze both jumped, startled. Just then the zookeeper, a cheerful young man named Jason, emerged from a side room and laughed when he saw the girls' reactions.

"I've never quite gotten used to the lion's roar, either," he said, still smiling.

Natalie pressed close to him, a look of longing on her face. "May I touch him, Jason? I've never seen a lion before. Please?"

This time it was the zookeeper's turn to be startled. "You want to touch the lion?"

"He's like a big cat to Natalie," Dianna explained. "She loves cats more than anything."

Jason looked at Tory and Breeze. Tory raised her eyebrows questioningly.

"Hm-m-m," he murmured, scratching his head. "Maybe there's a way to do this."

He disappeared into the zoo kitchen. When he returned, he carried a large piece of meat in one hand and a bowl filled with rabbit food in the other. "I'll make a deal with you, ladies," Jason said. He placed the bowl in Natalie's hands. She reached into it, picking up several of the tiny pellets and turning them over and over in her fingers, sniffing them, and even touching the tip of her tongue to one of them to taste it.

"That's not for you to eat, Natalie," he laughed. "It's for the guinea pigs and the rabbits." After leading the group across the room to an enclosure for the fluffy creatures, he found safe, comfortable places for each of them and gave them a handful of the tiny pellets to feed to the animals. "You girls feed these critters for me, and I'll feed Old Nero, the lion." He held the hunk of meat up. "Once he's fed and happy, I'll try to get him to lean his back against the fence so you can touch his fur safely. Is it a deal?"

"Yes!" the girls said in unison, holding their handfuls of feed down low. In soft voices they coaxed the animals to come and eat the pellets.

A guinea pig with a bright, calico pattern scurried close to Marie's outstretched hand. She giggled as she felt the furry paws touch her fingers. "He likes me," she exclaimed, her face wreathed in smiles. Then her expression became sober. "Maybe he's blind, too, and can't see me. Usually when people can see me, they don't like me."

Tory slipped close to her side and put her arm around the girl. "What makes you say that, Marie?" she asked gently.

The child's lips quivered and tears formed in her eyes. "All of my brothers and sisters have dark skin," she said. "My mom and dad are both Black. All the kids tease me because I have white skin and white hair. But the other kids with white skin don't like me because they say I have Black features."

Tory squeezed her shoulder, then glanced up to see Breeze watching her, a somber expression on her face.

"It sounds like you've had a lot of hurtful things happen to you, Marie," Tory said.

The tears welled up and spilled down the child's cheeks. She snuggled close to her like a lonely puppy.

"I couldn't help the color of skin I was born with, Tory," Marie said forlornly. "If people got mad at me because I was acting mean or bad, I could understand that. But why do they get mad at me because of what color I am?"

"I don't know," Tory replied. A large lump formed in her throat, making it hard for her to swallow. "All I know is *I* think you're beautiful just as you are, inside and out. Anyone that chooses not to see that is just missing out, that's all there is to it."

Marie sighed. "Do you think Jesus can see me?"

"I'm sure He can."

"Do you think He loves me even if I'm blind and my colors are all mixed up?"

Hugging the girl close, Tory replied, "I *know* He does."

Smiling, Marie pulled herself loose. She reached for the guinea pig, feeding him the pellets one by one.

Tory stood and backed away from Marie to stand next to Breeze. Together they watched the child in silence. Then Breeze spoke, her voice tight. "It hurts to see them suffer like they do, doesn't it?"

Tory looked at her, startled, remembering the courage her campers had displayed all week in their activities. She hadn't thought of them as suffering.

"I mean the rejection," Breeze explained. "Like Marie. She didn't ask for the situation she's in. Why do people have to be so cruel?"

"I don't know."

"My little sister is blind," Breeze said quietly. "I used to beat up other kids when they teased her. They had no idea how much they were hurting her, how much she just wanted to be like everybody else." She shook her head sadly. "I found out after a while that I couldn't change the attitudes of the whole world, much as I'd like to!"

Just then Marie called Tory to come over and pet her guinea pig. Breeze nodded in the blind girl's direction. "Go on, Tory. I'm going back to my cabin. I'll see you later." She headed for the door of the nature center, then turned to wave to Tory. "We missed you at our prayer group this week. We're praying especially for LeAnne and for Jake."

"Thanks, Breeze." Tory smiled to herself as the girl disappeared around the corner. Now she understood why she had sensed special inner strength in Breeze. She had faced some difficult challenges in life, having a blind child in her family.

Tory sat down on the floor close to Marie. While the girl played with the guinea pig, she let her thoughts wander back over the week with her blind campers. Every evening, before going to bed, she'd gathered the group together for worship. The girls had listened intently to stories about Jesus' life.

They seem like thirsty sponges, Father, Tory thought. *They need you so much. How can one week possibly make a difference?*

Sitting in the cedar shavings of the enclosure, her arms wrapped around her knees and her eyes shut, Tory prayed for each of the girls. Marie, who already bore more scars from cruelty and rejection than most adults have had to face. Bob, living in the shadow of the son her father never had. Carmen, who the other girls envied because she could have all the candy she wanted in her father's store, but who still hungered for the things in life that could really satisfy her. Angelina, the musician, rich in talent and in love. Judy, shy and softspoken, but full of insights about life. Natalie, lover of animals. And Dianna, independent spitfire.

Give me wisdom, Father. Love them through me. And thank you for loving me through them.

The door to the outer cages slammed. Tory opened her eyes to see Jason standing in the middle of the room, a grin of triumph on his face. "Come on, campers. Old Nero has consented to let you touch him."

Tory helped the girls out of the enclosure. They all held hands in a chain and followed Jason outside. The old lion lay sprawled against the chain link fence.

"All of you stand back with Tory," he ordered. "One by one, I'll take you close and help you put your hand on Nero's fur. He's toothless, so he can't bite you, but he still has some pretty sharp claws. We need to be careful."

Jason led Natalie to the fence first. She reached out to touch the coarse fur, a rapturous expression on her face.

"I touched a lion," she murmured over and over as he brought her back to the group. "I really touched a lion."

Later that night, after the Saturday evening campfire program ended, Tory gathered the girls for one last worship time together. Angelina played her wooden flute. The haunting notes of "Amazing Grace" floated on the air as if they had a life of their own.

"It's story time now!" Dianna announced when Angelina finished her song.

Tory cleared her throat. "All week I've been telling you the story of Jesus," she began. "How He came to earth as a tiny baby. How Satan, Jesus' enemy since before the world was created, used a wicked king to try to kill Him, but God sent an angel to warn His parents to take Him far away. We've talked about His miracles and the way He treated the children with love and respect, even when others were pushing them away. And we've talked about how He valued people from cultures and family backgrounds that others considered bad and unworthy. With all the good that Jesus did, the people still killed him by nailing Him up on a cross. But three days later He came back to life.

"When He died, Jesus' followers were very sad. They knew about the terrible war between Jesus and Satan. It looked like Satan had won. But when Jesus came out of that tomb, alive, they then knew Satan would *never* win.

"Jesus went back to heaven, but He told us that we can talk to Him whenever we want to, that He will send His spirit of love to live inside us if we want it. He told us that He will come back soon to take us to heaven with Him where there won't be any more diseases that take eyesight away. The lions won't have to be caged up. We can ride them if we want to!"

Slipping out of her place in the circle, Dianna squeezed in next to Tory. Taking her counselor's hand, she peered up into her face. "Tory," she whispered, "I want to have Jesus' spirit of love in my heart. How can I do that? Can you ask Him to do that for me? I know you talk to Him a lot."

Tory hugged her close. "I'd be glad to talk to Him for you, Dianna, but you can do it yourself, you know."

"But how do I know He'll hear me? He doesn't even know me."

"Yes, He does. He's known you since before you were born. He knows everything about you."

Dianna looked thoughtful. "Does He know I'm blind?"

"Yes. He knows that, too."

"Well, if He loves me and knows I'm blind, why didn't He make my eyes better like He did those people in the story?"

Tory's mind raced. *Father, help me with this one,* she prayed. *I need some wisdom here.*

"I have something I want to explain to all of you," she said, finally. "Dianna's question is a good one. It's one that lots of people ask when hurtful things happen.

"I don't know all the answers either, but I have learned some things by studying the Bible. The Bible is God's special book. It tells us everything we need to know about God and Jesus and heaven." Pausing, Tory took a deep breath. "The Bible tells us that we're caught in that same war that Jesus fought with Satan. It's still going on today and will keep going until Jesus comes to give us our new bodies.

"Even though Jesus won the war, Satan is still fighting against us for a little while longer. He knows how much Jesus loves us, so he tries to hurt Jesus by hurting us. Satan brought so much disease and suffering on the earth through the centuries that all of us in one way or another are hurt by it. Does that make sense to you?"

The girls nodded, their faces solemn. Tory continued.

"Sometimes God *does* heal us from our diseases or handicaps and sometimes He teaches us *through* our handicaps things that we may never have learned another way."

Angelina's hand shot up in the air. "I can hear better than any of my friends," she said, excitement in her voice. "Because I can't see, I have to use my ears, nose, and hands to make up for my eyes."

"Exactly. That works in the spiritual area, too. Sometimes, because of the hard things we have to go through, we *see* things with our hearts that we would have completely missed out on otherwise. We learn to trust God and to really love others."

Natalie sighed wistfully. "I'll be glad to get my new body when Jesus comes. I want to ride a lion and be able to see where I'm going."

Dianna tugged at Tory's sleeve. "You didn't finish telling me how I could have Jesus in my heart."

"I want to know, too," Carmen added.

"Me, too," Marie echoed.

"OK. Any of you that want to, can pray with me. Let's close our eyes and talk to God."

The girls snickered, and Tory realized with chagrin that it made no difference whether they closed their eyes or not since they couldn't see anyway.

"Dear Father, I know that even when I'm good it can't make up for the wrong I've done. And that without Jesus' spirit of love inside me, my heart is blinded by selfishness. I ask for Jesus' presence in my life to wash away the wrong and give my heart eyes to see Your ways. Thank You for the promise You gave in Your word that when we call out for You, You will answer. We love You. In Jesus' name, Amen."

When the prayer ended, Dianna sighed. "I'm so glad I came to ride horses and swim and learn to shoot a bow and arrow. But learning to love Jesus has been the best part of camp. I can't wait to go home and tell my mom all about Him."

The other girls nodded in agreement.

"Group hug!" Bob shouted. Tory and all the girls squeezed together in one big hug.

"OK, in bed with all of you," Tory announced. "Time for lights-out. It's an early day tomorrow, getting the cabin cleaned out to go home."

Tory lay awake in her bunk long after the girls breathing deepened into light snores. She curled up on the edge of the bunk closest to the window and gazed up through the trees at a patch of sky sprinkled with stars.

Thank you, Father, she prayed. *Thanks for giving me the chance to reach out to these girls. Please go with them when they leave here. The world is such a cruel place sometimes.*

An owl hooted in a nearby tree. The sound of a coyote yipping at the moon echoed through the air. Tory shut her eyes tight and tried to imagine what it would be like to be blind. Never to see the blue sky or the face of a friend. Then she thought of Rob and the experience he'd had, looking at the sky and the flowers but seeing no color.

I could be blind even with eyes that see, she mused. And with that thought, she drifted off to sleep.

CHAPTER THIRTEEN

As Tory walked into the stable its familiar odors surrounded her. Allie stood in the doorway of the tack room, a bridle slung over her shoulder.

"Welcome back, Tory," the redheaded girl said, grinning. "We sure missed you around here." She glanced around furtively and lowered her voice to a whisper. "Especially Brian. He moped around like he'd lost his best friend. What is it with you guys?"

Tory felt herself blushing. "Nothing. There's nothing at all."

Allie shook her head. "You'd better tell *him* that." She pulled a saddle from its rack and headed down the corridor toward one of the end stalls.

A feeling of confusion threatened to overwhelm Tory. Why did Brian act the way he did? She wanted to believe that he considered her a special friend, but his behavior with other girls gave her a different impression.

Taking Blackberry's saddle from its place, Tory approached the roan mare's stall. "Hi, girl. It's me."

The mare nickered and took a step toward the stall door. Tory stopped still in her tracks. It was the first time the horse had shown any interest in being friends.

"Well, so you missed me, too, huh? Let's see what we can do together today."

Quietly Tory opened the stall door, making no attempt to hide the bridle, but left it hanging on her shoulder as she walked toward Blackberry, a carrot stub in her out-stretched palm.

Although the horse shied back against the stall wall, she didn't flatten her ears back or attempt to kick.

"Good girl," Tory said, keeping her voice even and calm. She moved in closer, holding her hand out in front of her. Cautiously Blackberry stretched and nibbled on the piece of carrot. Tory rubbed the soft place behind the horse's ears with her other hand.

As soon as Blackberry finished eating, Tory slipped the bit between the mare's teeth and the headstall of the bridle up over her head. Then she reached for the saddle blanket. The mare allowed her to place the thick soft pad on her back.

"You are turning into a real sweetie," Tory cooed as she reached for the saddle. "Maybe we'll get our act together in time for the rodeo. How do you feel about barrel racing?"

Abruptly she stepped back and looked at Blackberry with new eyes. Until now, she hadn't let herself hope for enough progress with Blackberry to be able to ride her in the rodeo.

"You're small with slender legs, but you're quick," she said softly. "You obviously have Arabian blood in you. That gives you your nervousness, but it also gives you a lot of heart. I think we can do this, you and I!"

After tightening Blackberry's cinch, Tory led her out to the hitching rail just as Brian and Mike walked across the archery range.

"Hey, kiddo!" the head wrangler shouted. "Glad to have you back. We held down the fort, but it wasn't the same without you."

She smiled and waved at him, then turned her attention back to Blackberry, ignoring Brian altogether.

"OK girl, let's do it right this time." She positioned the reins, slipped the toe of her boot into the stirrup of

Blackberry's saddle, and swung onto the mare's back.

The mare stood quivering for a moment. Tory held her breath, waiting for the explosion. But it never came.

"Come on, girl," she said, squeezing her legs into the mare's sides and clucking to her. Blackberry took a cautious step forward. "Good girl." Tory patted the horse's neck. "Let's take a walk down to the airstrip."

Once out in the open, Tory worked with Blackberry on neck reining, urging her into figure eight patterns and large circles. Though hesitant at first, the mare seemed to catch on quickly to what Tory expected of her.

"You *do* have a lot of heart," the girl whispered.

The lessons continued every day during the next few weeks. When she wasn't busy with trail rides or helping keep the stable clean, Tory saddled Blackberry and practiced left and right turns, stopping, backing up, and lead changes with her. The little mare no longer flattened herself against the back wall of her stall when Tory approached, but she still refused to let Brian or Mike touch her.

"I guess we won't use Blackberry in the Nativity skit next week," Brian joked one day, after trying to get close to the little mare. "She'd probably wheel around and accidentally kick Baby Jesus while trying to nail Joseph."

Mike shook his head. "It's too bad. I'm sure it must have been a man that mistreated her, the way she reacts to men."

"How's LeAnne today?" Tory asked, changing the subject.

"She feels better, but she's still having a lot of trouble with nausea." Mike sighed. "It's hard to believe this is happening to us. LeAnne has always been so healthy. She has a doctor's appointment in two weeks. We'll know then if she's strong enough for surgery."

"Do you think she'd mind if I dropped in sometime today to say hi?" Tory asked.

Mike shook his head. "Of course not. She'd love to

see you. In fact, let's go check on her right now."

Tory followed him across the field to the little flat-topped bungalow.

"LeAnne, you've got company," he called, pushing open the front door.

His wife sat in the middle of the living-room floor, the huge piggy bank in her lap. She smiled up at them as they walked into the room.

"Just in time. I think we should break the piggy bank today."

"What?" Tory looked at her in surprise. "Why do you want to do that?"

Mike and LeAnne exchanged knowing glances, then he explained. "We want to get contacts for Allie. Do you remember our last practice for the Nativity skit? Allie makes a great angel, but she was self-conscious about her glasses. What angel wears glasses? But when she took them off, she couldn't see anything."

LeAnne shook the huge bank.

"Besides, she has a birthday coming up. What better way to spend all this change?" Clearly pleased with the idea, she smiled to herself.

Mike rummaged around in one of the kitchen drawers and came up with an old hammer. Holding it up, he grinned.

"I think this will do the job." He smashed it down on the porcelain bank. Then he handed the hammer to LeAnne, who delivered another crashing blow. Soon the bank lay in fragments on the floor, revealing a huge pile of pennies, nickels, dimes, and quarters.

"Want to help count?" Mike asked Tory.

She sat cross-legged on the floor and helped them sort the change into piles. LeAnne stuffed the money into paper tubes the bank had given her. Soon stacks of neatly rolled coins lay on the floor among the shards from the broken bank.

"There," LeAnne said, a satisfied tone in her voice. "Now I just need to take Allie into town to get her fitted for contacts. Tory, could you see if she's free this afternoon?"

"Are you sure you're up to doing this?" her husband asked.

"Yes. I feel better today and want to get out."

Tory stood. "I'll go find Allie. I'm sure she'll be glad to take a trip to town."

LeAnne held her hand up as the girl started for the door. "Don't tell her why we're going. I want to surprise her."

That afternoon Tory cleaned stalls and helped Mike oil down bridles. She could tell by the furrow above his eyebrows that he was worried about LeAnne. It was the first time she had ever done chores with him that he didn't whistle while he worked.

"I should never have let her go to town by herself," he muttered, looking at his watch for the hundredth time. "It's almost 5:00. Buying contacts shouldn't take this long."

Pulling the heavy wooden ladder from its place under the eaves of the barn, he positioned it against the edge of the loft. "I'm going up to see if I can find anything we can use for props in our Nativity scene," he announced, climbing nimbly up the rough ladder.

Brian emerged from one of the stalls. As he watched the head wrangler disappear into the loft, he leaned over to Tory. "He's trying to keep himself distracted until LeAnne gets back," he whispered. "He knows there's nothing usable up there."

Tory nodded. She picked up the end of the garden hose coiled just outside the barn entrance. "I think I'll spray down the sand. It's pretty dusty around here."

As she reached for the spigot handle to turn the water on, a shiny black spider darted out from behind the handle and ran down the top of the hose. Fascinated, Tory grabbed a twig and flipped the spider over on her back, only to gasp as she saw the bright red hourglass pattern on the spider's abdomen.

"Brian, come here. Quick!"

He rushed to her side. When he saw the spider, he immediately crushed it with his boot.

"Black widow," he said, an ominous tone in his voice. "Deadly poisonous."

She shuddered. "And I almost grabbed it with my bare hand."

A shake of his head. "I guess your guardian angel is looking out for you."

Tory stared at the crumpled black body on the ground, the red hourglass still visible. "Whew," she said, her heart still pounding, "I'm sure glad he is."

Brian took her hand and looked into her eyes, a strange expression on his face. "I'm glad he is, too. I don't know what I'd do if something happened to you."

Her face flushing, she pulled her hand gently away from Brian's and turned the water on to spray the barn corridor. Just then she heard the sound of LeAnne's car coming up the drive to the stable.

When Allie stepped from the car, Tory whistled in amazement. The girl's long red hair had been pulled back with a hair tie. Her eyes were large and luminous, like a deer's, framed by thick lashes. "Allie, you look *fabulous*."

"Yep," Brian chuckled. "That's the angel look if I ever saw it."

Clearly embarrassed by all the attention, the girl smiled shyly. Just then LeAnne stepped from the car, a strange look on her face.

"Where's Mike?" she asked.

Tory and Brian pointed up to the loft. LeAnne stood at the base of the ladder and called up to him. "Hey, Mike. You'd better come down. I've got something to tell you."

Mike's muffled voice answered from somewhere in the back of the loft. It sounded as if he said something like "Just a minute. I'm busy."

LeAnne put her hands on her hips and yelled again. "Hey, Papa, I think you'd better get down here before this baby thinks he has no father."

"W-what did you say?" Mike's face appeared over the edge of the loft, his eyes wide.

"I said, you're a daddy." His wife's shoulders shook with laughter. "I stopped to see the doctor while Allie and I were in town. He told me something didn't seem right with this 'growth,' so he listened to it with a stethoscope and heard a heartbeat. I don't have cancer—I'm pregnant!"

Tory felt her heart skip a beat. LeAnne pregnant? She thought back over the previous few weeks and pictured LeAnne's pale face, nauseated and miserable. Of course! It had been morning sickness all along.

Allie grabbed the hose from Tory's hand and directed the spray straight up at Mike. "Baby shower, baby shower!" she chanted, soaking his clothes.

The head wrangler climbed down the ladder, drenched and bewildered. He held LeAnne at arm's length, looking at her in amazement.

"A baby?" he choked out the words. "We're really going to have a baby?"

LeAnne nodded, tears in her eyes, then she and Mike headed arm in arm back to the bungalow, leaving the car where it sat.

Father, You are truly awesome, Tory thought as she watched the couple walk away, engrossed in happy conversation. *Your ways are truly beyond anything we could ever dream of.*

CHAPTER FOURTEEN

Sabbath morning dawned bright and clear. As Tory stretched and yawned, rubbing the sleep from her eyes, suddenly she remembered that it was the day of the Nativity-scene skit.

Many of the campers' families were expected to arrive today, along with visitors from the community, to see the different departments of the camp act out Jesus' life.

Grabbing her bright-blue robe with its tasseled belt and creamy-white head scarf, Tory ran down the path toward the stable. Allie joined her, a pair of gold-sequined wings and a halo under her arm.

"So you overslept, too?" the redheaded girl grinned at her.

Tory nodded. "My alarm didn't go off. If it hadn't been for Nero's roars, I'd still be asleep."

Mike and Brian bent over a rough wooden manger set up in the largest box stall in the barn. A few strategically placed nails, and the manger stood, sturdy and strong, awaiting Baby Jesus.

The head wrangler filled the interior of the manger with hay and scattered the rest of the bale around the stall, then stuffed the baling twine into his pockets. Two bales of hay formed seats on either side of the manger.

In another stall he and Brian had placed an old table with some chairs. A clay lamp sat on the table, looking for all the world as if it had appeared directly from a peasant's home in old Judea. The outside walls of the stable were only about five-feet high, leaving a four-foot opening between the top of the wall and the roof. Mike propped a wooden bench against the wall outside the stall so Allie could make her angelic appearance in the opening.

Just as Tory slipped into the tack room to don her costume, she spotted LeAnne hurrying to the barn, a bundle in her arms. She could see a doll's face amid the white wrappings. LeAnne wore a pretty white smock, printed with the word "Baby" and an arrow pointing down to her abdomen. Tory smiled to herself. How perfect that LeAnne should provide baby Jesus for the skit.

The first group of campers had already arrived when Tory emerged from the tack room. She wore the white scarf over her head, with the ends wrapped around her neck and tossed back over the shoulder of her long blue gown. Barefoot, she padded to the stall with the table and lamp.

Mike sat at the table, a scroll and quill in his hand. He looked up, smiling, when he saw Tory.

"Mary, my daughter, where have you been?"

Tory bowed her head respectfully.

"To the market, Father, to search for the cloth for my wedding gown. I want to be sure it is beautiful enough for Joseph to notice it well."

"Ah," Mike said, standing and placing his arm around her waist. "You are a good daughter who brings me much pride and joy."

Then Mike slipped from the stall. As Tory removed her scarf and prepared to lie down to "sleep" for the next scene, she glanced at the audience peering over the stall wall from "bleachers" Mike had constructed. Jake's face appeared among the campers.

Tory lay down on a hay-bale bed in the corner of the stall and closed her eyes. Allie's head and shoulders "appeared" above the outside wall, her radiant face framed by golden wings and a gossamer white gown. A sparkling crown rested on her head. Tory's mouth dropped open in amazement. The girl truly looked like an angel.

"Blessed are you, Mary, among all women," Allie said, her voice smooth and flowing. "God has chosen you to be the mother of His Son. His Spirit will overshadow you and the baby you will have will be the Saviour of the world, the Messiah that you have all waited for."

Instantly Tory sat straight up, her eyes wide.

"Don't be afraid," Allie continued. "God is with you." As quickly as she had appeared, she now vanished.

Tory slipped out of the stall, then returned a short time later. Mike sat at the table again, lighting the clay lamp.

"Father," she said, her eyes lowered, "I have something I need to talk to you about. Something perplexing but wonderful."

The head wrangler stood and turned toward her, placing his hands on her shoulders. "What is it, my child? You can tell me anything. You know that."

"I'm pregnant, Father. But the baby isn't Joseph's, it's God's."

Mike dropped his hands to his sides. "What?" he roared. "What kind of insanity is this? What kind of girl are *you?*" He paced the interior of the stall, wringing his hands. "Get out of my sight," he said in disgust. "I don't want to see your face again."

Mike left and Tory threw herself onto her "bed," sobbing bitterly. Just then Brian entered the stall. Sitting down beside her, he patted her on the back.

"What is it, Mary? Why are you crying?"

"Oh, Joseph," she wailed, "I'm pregnant. The angel came and told me I'm to be the mother of the Messiah. Father doesn't believe me. You believe me, don't you?"

He jumped to his feet, backing away from Tory as if she had a contagious disease. Without a word, he turned and fled through the stall door, leaving Tory to weep bitterly alone in her room.

The scene changed again and Brian, in another stall arranged as if it were a Jewish home, lay down to sleep. From her place on the straw bed, Tory could hear Brian's "snoring." Then Allie's voice declared, "Joseph, don't be afraid to take Mary as your wife. She's told the truth. Her baby *is* the Messiah, and you are to call His name Jesus."

Tory sat up on the straw just in time to see Brian rush into the stall. He threw his arms around her, hugging her tight, saying, "Oh, Mary. I'm sorry I didn't believe you. Can you ever forgive me?"

The smell of Brian's aftershave filled her nose. *This is not Brian hugging me,* she reminded herself sternly. *This is Joseph. And, for right now, I am Mary.*

In the next scene, Tory sat sideways on Merrilegs' back, a pillow stuffed under her gown to make it look as if she was far advanced in her pregnancy. Brian led Merrilegs slowly down the corridor, knocking on stall doors as he went.

"Do you have room for a couple of strangers from Nazareth?" Brian asked as LeAnne opened one of the doors. "See, my wife is about to have a baby. Her labor pains have already started."

Tory groaned and lay over Merrilegs' neck to illustrate the point. LeAnne slammed the door shut, saying, "No! No room for the likes of you. Go sleep in the street."

Mike opened another door in answer to Brian's knock. "What do you want," he snarled. "It's late and I was already in bed."

Brian bowed low. "My humblest apologies, kind sir. But my wife is in labor. We've traveled far and need a place for her to lie down. The baby could come any time."

The man let his face soften as he listened to Brian's story. "There's no room in this building, but you may stay in the stable out back. At least you'll have fresh straw to sleep on."

After Brian led Merrilegs to the large box stall with the rough little manger, he helped Tory dismount and eased her down onto a pile of hay.

Suddenly, Allie appeared in the opening above the stall, shouting, "Glory to God in the Highest, and on earth, peace and good will to men."

While the camper's attention was focused on the girl, Tory slipped the baby Jesus doll from under the hay and cradled it in her arms. She laid it gently into the manger, singing a soft lullaby as Brian stood by, leaning on his staff.

The scene over, Tory and Brian waited for the campers to leave before they slipped out of the box stall to arrange the props in the other stalls for the next batch of campers to come.

"I like the way they divided the campers into groups to visit each reenactment," Brian said. "This way they can see the skit unfolding better than if a whole mob came in here at once."

Tory nodded in agreement. "I just wish we could see the other scenes," she said wistfully. "I hear the baptism of Jesus down at the waterfront is a gripping scene, not to mention the crucifixion."

Then she paused, listening. She held her hand up for silence as Allie joined them, her sequins sparkling even in the dim interior of the barn. A strange sound came from somewhere near the barn. Tory tiptoed by each stall, peering into them as she passed. All were empty. Mike and Brian had turned all the horses unnecessary for the skit out to pasture for *their* Sabbath rest.

Once outside, Tory followed the sound around the front of the barn. There, under the eave, stood Jake. His shoulders shook in deep heaving sobs as he leaned against the side of the building. Tory stepped quickly to his side and put her arms around him as he cried. When Jake calmed down, she listened as he talked.

"It never hit me personally before just what Jesus did to come to this earth as a baby," he said, his voice still shaking. "I watched you playing Mary, with your father yelling at you, and it struck me—these were real people. People who hurt and were cold, hungry, and tired. People who felt rejection and disappointment. I realized in that moment that Jesus knows all about the pain in my past. He experienced it too."

Jake wiped his face and looked her straight in the eye. He seemed to be struggling for words. Finally, he said solemnly, "I've given my life to Him, Tory. All of it. For better or for worse. I want what you and Rob have."

Suddenly she felt warm tears of her own slipping down her cheeks. "You won't regret it," she said, smiling through her tears. "It's the adventure of a lifetime. You'll see."

Jake slipped his arm through hers. "I can't wait," he said as they walked around the corner to the hitching area. He gave her a quick hug. "See you later. I'm off to the waterfront to watch the baptism scene. I want to see how it's done, since I'll be next."

Tory laughed and waved goodbye. She watched him saunter across the field toward the spring, shaking her head in wonder. "Who'd have ever guessed?" she whispered under her breath. Allie and Brian joined her, standing in the sand, staring after Jake.

"What was that all about?" Brian asked, a puzzled look on his face. "Was he making that noise?"

"That was another one of God's miracles at work right under our own noses," Tory explained. "It happened while he watched our skit. Jake just surrendered his life to the Lord!"

"Wow," Allie said quietly. "Haven't you and Rob had him on your prayer list all summer?"

"Yep." Suddenly Tory realized that all three of the main requests on her prayer list had now been answered. None of them in exactly the way she had in mind, but all of them clearly in God's perfect timing.

She'd asked for a horse to ride and God had helped her win Blackberry's trust. Although she'd prayed for an adopted baby for Mike and LeAnne, now they were expecting their very own. And she'd asked for God to work in Jake's heart and He had, in a wonderful, unexpected way.

Well, Father, You outdid yourself again. But then, why am I so surprised?

CHAPTER FIFTEEN

I can't believe the summer's almost gone." Allie sat on a bucket in the tack room with her chin in her hands, looking forlorn.

Tory reached over her, pulling Blackberry's bridle from its peg. "I know. It seems like yesterday we were preparing for our first group of campers. Now, tomorrow is our last day with them."

"And tomorrow night is the rodeo!" Allie's eyes shone with anticipation. "Mayonnaise is ready. How's Blackberry?"

Tory shrugged. "She does great when I work her alone, with no distractions. Who knows what she'll do with a noisy, cheering crowd and so much other commotion."

She hoisted the mare's saddle from its rack. "I'm taking Blackberry out for a while. Is there anything you need before I go?"

Allie shook her head. "Just a few more months of summer. I'm not ready for school to start again." She looked at Tory quizzically. "Where are you going to college this fall?"

"I'm going to a little community college near my parents' home in Missouri. I can't afford to go back to a boarding college. It won't be the same as attending a Christian college, but I hear their nurses' training is good. I want to be a nurse like LeAnne."

Allie made a face. "Ugh. I can't stand the sight of blood. Or needles."

"Well, I'm a little worried about the needles myself. I can't imagine giving anyone a shot." Tory shuddered at the thought. "But LeAnne says you get used to it. She's been a nurse for a long time, so I guess she should know."

Blackberry poked her head over the stall door and nickered to Tory. "OK, OK," she laughed, "I'm coming."

Tory saddled and bridled the horse and rode her out into the arena to practice maneuvering around the barrels. The mare leaned into the turns and sped around them as agilely as a cat. Her slender legs flew on the return stretch. Tory didn't have a stopwatch, but she was fairly certain Blackberry's time was fast enough to beat any horse in the barn.

The moon rose full and bright on Saturday night, and the horses pranced with excitement, full of energy after their Sabbath rest from trail rides. Tory smoothed the front of her red shirt, tucking it neatly into her jeans. A red and white bandanna hung from her neck.

"Come on, staff," Mike called, wiping the perspiration from his forehead. "Let's have a prayer together before we start the rodeo."

Tory, Allie, Brian, Mike, and LeAnne, all dressed in red shirts and jeans, joined hands and bowed their heads for prayer.

"Father," Mike prayed, "we dedicate this rodeo to You, asking your protection on the campers and on our staff. Help us to show these kids that life with You is adventurous and fun. We love you. Amen."

"Amen," Tory whispered.

"Time for the grand entrance," Brian announced. He disappeared into the tack room and returned with an armload of colorful, full-sized flags. After handing Tory an American flag, he then distributed the others to Mike, LeAnne, Allie, and several other staff members who were riding.

Campers lined the corral fence. Some perched on the top rail, others peeked through the slats. One of the lifeguards sat in the announcer's booth, holding a microphone. A lively march blared over the loudspeaker.

Tory led Blackberry to the hitching rail where Allie sat, already mounted on Mayonnaise, a Christian flag in her hand.

"Good, I'm glad you're here," Tory said. "Could you hold my flag while I mount up? The fluttering spooks Blackberry."

Mayonnaise stood calmly while Allie reached for Tory's flag. The billowing flags flapping against his body didn't seem to faze him. Once Tory settled into position in the saddle, Allie handed the American flag back to her.

Tory held the flag as high as she could, away from Blackberry's body, but a breeze caught the material and flipped one corner of the flag under Blackberry's flank. Tory felt the mare's muscles tense. Blackberry rocked backward, her eyes rolling in fear.

"Easy, girl. Easy." She kept her voice calm, but she felt anything but calm inside.

Brian, mounted on Bullet, slipped up beside Blackberry and grabbed her reins. He spoke to the mare gently, holding her steady until she stopped trembling.

"Are you all right?" he asked Tory, a concerned expression on his face. "It looked like she was about to supply the fireworks for the rodeo. I thought I'd better intervene."

"Thanks, I was a little worried there for a minute myself."

Holding his flag high, he poked the end of the flagpole into the hole just behind the pommel of his saddle. Tory did the same with hers. Then she reined Blackberry up beside Bullet and waited for the others.

Jake, seated on Barney, pulled into line beside Allie

and Mayonnaise. He, too, carried a Christian flag. Tory smiled as she watched him handle Barney. During the past few weeks Jake had spent a lot of time at the stable working with Barney, and it showed. Breeze had accompanied him several times, her silvery laugh echoing through the barn. Tory liked seeing them together. Now that Jake's attitude had changed they seemed a perfect match.

Mike on Toby and LeAnne on Jasmine followed Jake and Allie in the line. Each of them held a Florida state flag. Mike motioned to Brian to start the procession and two by two the horses pranced toward the arena gate.

Suddenly a colorful shape darted past the line of horses and riders. The crowd of campers roared as Merrilegs galloped into the arena, bright ribbons and streamers tied to his mane and tail. Red and purple rings circled his eyes. A long-legged clown teetered precariously on his back, his bulbous red nose shining in the spotlight. The clown wore baggy overalls with purple polka-dotted suspenders and a huge yellow bow tie. A red curly wig covered his head.

Tory watched the clown, laughing with the others. Then the clown fell off Merrilegs' back and rolled immediately into two back flips.

"Rob!" Tory whispered under her breath, not wanting to give his secret away to the campers. She had seen him do his acrosports routine on the lawn down by the spring. He was the only guy in the camp that could do back flips.

Just as the clown intercepted Merrilegs and sprinted from the arena, Brian signaled the line of riders and nudged Bullet into an easy canter. Tory stayed close beside him, holding the flag upright as Blackberry galloped.

Two by two the riders circled the arena. Then they turned toward the center, splitting off with girls going one way and guys the other. Meeting at one end, the couples joined again, each pair executing a figure-eight in a different corner of the arena. Then the group lined up together in the center. The riders held their flags high and waved their hats at the cheering crowd. With a great flourish they galloped out through the gate.

Tory handed her flag to Brian and patted Blackberry's sweat-drenched neck. "You were fabulous, little mare," she said softly. "That would have been hard work even for a well-trained horse. I'm proud of you."

Brian pulled Bullet up close beside her. "She *is* a well-trained horse. *You're* the one who's done a great job. That little horse was green as clover just two months ago."

Feeling her face grow hot, Tory murmured, "Thanks," and reined Blackberry back toward the arena.

Mike stood at one end of the huge corral, holding a pile of rough burlap feed bags in his arms.

"All right, campers," the announcer began. "We need six volunteers to run the cracker race."

Several dozen children waved their hands frantically, hoping to be picked. Counselors and other staff who sat along the fence helped choose six campers from among the group. Mike gave each camper a burlap bag and instructed them to climb inside.

"You must stay inside your bag," the announcer continued. "Hop down to the other end of the arena. There a staff member will give you some crackers. The first person to whistle out loud after chewing the cracker wins. On your marks, get set, go!"

The campers lining the fence laughed hysterically as those hopping in the burlap bags fell over each other trying to reach the other side of the arena. A little girl with dark pigtails was the first to shove the crackers into her mouth. She tried to whistle, but only dry cracker crumbs came out. Then she chewed and chewed and tried again. This time she was able to whistle a tune. The audience clapped and cheered for her.

Other races followed. Tory doubled over with laughter as several staff members fell into the watering tank during the apple dunking contest. Then Mike and Brian cleared the arena and rolled three barrels into a triangle pattern for the barrel race.

"It's time, little one," Tory said, tightening Blackberry's cinch strap. "Let's show 'em what you can do."

Brian led Bullet through the gate into the arena where he waited just behind the starting line for the other contestants to arrive. Allie rode in on Mayonnaise and Jake on Barney. The crowd erupted into laughter when Merrilegs trotted into the arena with Rob, still dressed as a clown, sitting backward in the saddle.

"Wait a minute," the announcer said. "This is a serious race. You can't ride backward in this event."

Rob crossed his arms, holding his red nose high in the air, acting as if his feelings were hurt. Then he flipped around on Merrilegs' back and galloped around the barrels going the wrong direction. "Hey," the announcer shouted in mock alarm, "that's the wrong way. I'll have to take a two-minute penalty off your time."

Rob pulled Merrilegs to a sudden stop, jumped from his back, and ran around the barrels on foot. Tory slipped Blackberry into the arena and stood behind Jake while the campers shouted with laughter at Rob's antics.

"Well, now that Bozo here has shown us how *not* to run the barrels, let's see how the professionals do it," the announcer said. "First in line tonight is Brian Winters on the magnificent Bullet."

Mike stood beside the announcer, a cap gun in his hand. He pulled the trigger and the cap exploded with a sharp *crack!* Bullet leaped from the starting point as if he'd been shot from the gun himself.

Brian crouched low in the saddle, reining Bullet around the first barrel to the right. He made a cloverleaf turn and circled the second barrel to the left. Rounding the third barrel, he shouted to Bullet, urging him into a dead run.

"Wow!" The announcer gushed. "Eighteen seconds. Great time for Brian Winters."

Jake rode next on Barney. Breeze, perched on the top rail of the fence near the starting point, clapped and cheered for him. Jake tipped his hat to her and grinned broadly. Tory marveled at the speed Jake was able to coax from the albino gelding, but he knocked one of the barrels over, increasing his total time to 26 seconds.

"You go ahead," Allie whispered to Tory, holding Mayonnaise back. "I'm not going to race him tonight."

With a nod Tory reined Blackberry into place. The gun fired, and she squeezed hard on Blackberry to run her fastest.

The little roan mare leaped into action, ignoring the shouting crowd. Her slim legs churned up the sand as she ran, spinning around the barrels in perfect form. Once on the homestretch, Tory shouted in her ear, "Go, Blackberry, give it all you've got."

"Fantastic!" The announcer stood staring at his stopwatch. "Seventeen seconds flat. Tory Butler and Blackberry are the winners of our barrel racing contest tonight!"

After the rodeo that night she walked the mare back to her stall where she brushed her down and cleaned her hooves carefully. The mare stood quietly while Tory picked up each of her hooves.

Brian's face appeared over the stall door. "That doesn't even seem like the same horse you started training this summer. You sure have a knack with horses."

Tory pulled a tangle from Blackberry's mane. "Thanks, Brian," she replied softly. "I learned a lot of it from watching you."

"Could we take a walk? I really need to talk to you."

Nodding, she gave Blackberry one last pat and returned the currycomb to the tack room.

A warm breeze rustled the grass in the field as they walked down the path toward camp.

"Tory," he said, his voice choked, "I don't know how to say this, but I want to ask you to marry me. I haven't thought of anything else for weeks. Do you care about me at all?"

She stopped in her tracks and stared at him. "Are you serious?"

"Yes. Completely serious."

Slowly Tory shook her head, her emotions tumbling over each other in mass confusion. All last winter, when she was away at college, she'd dreamed of this moment. She thought of the pain of seeing him with Brooke this summer. Then she remembered her new plans for her education. God was calling her to some kind of work for Him in the medical field.

"Thank you, Brian," she said finally. "I *do* care about you, and I'm honored that you want to marry me. But I can't. I'm not ready for that kind of commitment."

A pained look flitted through his eyes, then he put his arm around her shoulder and squeezed.

"I understand," he said finally. "And I respect your decision. Maybe someday the timing will be better."

Tears filled her eyes. "God's timing is always perfect," she said, somehow managing a smile. "I'm glad He brought me here so I could see Jake surrender his life to Christ and LeAnne's miracle pregnancy. I know everything else will work out, too."

He squeezed her shoulder again.

"Mike was right about you. You *are* an amazing woman."

Tory shook her head. "No. We have an amazing heavenly Father."

"OK," Brian laughed, "you win." He took the red handkerchief from his neck and tied it around her wrist.

"Just don't forget this wrangler summer and the guy whose heart you hold, OK?"

She stretched up and kissed him lightly on the cheek. "It's a deal. I won't forget."

Waving goodbye, she ambled back toward her cabin. She felt the swoosh of bat wings as the tiny creature dived close by her head in pursuit of an elusive insect. Old Nero roared from his cage in the zoo, and a chorus of frogs croaked a response from the edge of the spring.

Tory glanced back over her shoulder in the direction Brian had gone. She felt a tug at her heart as she pictured the expression of disappointment on his face when she refused his marriage proposal.

"Brian Winters," she whispered softly, "somehow I think God might have another chapter for us someday."

Her thoughts drifted back to her first day at Cool Springs Camp more than a year earlier and her prayer for a chance to work with the horses. She laughed and shook her head.

Father, she prayed, *life with You is an amazing experience. You've given me so much more than I even knew to ask for. What an incredible summer this has been.*

Glancing up at the sky, she caught her breath in wonder at the brilliant display of stars against the deep velvet canopy. She picked out the Big Dipper, Arcturus, and Vega, the brightest star in the summer Triangle.

It's all in your hands, isn't it, Father? She sighed. *The whole universe. And me. I love You.*

A bright star just overhead seemed to blink back in response, like a Morse code signal relayed from some distant heavenly place. And Tory was sure it said, *I love you, too.*

A Horse Called Mayonnaise

by JoAnne Chitwood Nowack

Ever since Tory heard about the horseback trip at camp she'd been unable to think of anything else. It was her reason for being there to work, almost her reason for "being" at all.

But now her dream's in big trouble. Gorgeous Jan Cole has signed up to go, and only two girls will be chosen. How can she compete against a girl who always seems to get everything based on her good looks?

Discouraged, Tory's ready to quit till a friend helps her see herself from God's point of view. When she decides to trust Him with her hopes, she's in for a summer beyond her wildest dreams. A summer that brings the thrill of a horse called Mayonnaise.

Paper, 124 pages.
US$7.99, Cdn$11.49